Somewhere in Between

Somewhere in Between

Behind every dream lies a deeper truth

A Novella
by Lilly Benton

Inspired by True Events

For my sister, Kristina—
my first co-author in imagination,
and always my safe place.

PART I

The Weight of Beauty & Love

Chapter One

CHAPTER ONE

The ballroom shimmered under candlelight, casting a warm, flattering glow that softened edges and made everyone feel effortlessly glamorous. It was deliberate, our signature touch. Crystal bowls overflowed with graceful calla lilies, their slender stems arching elegantly above lush clusters of blush-colored peonies. Tables dressed in pristine white linens caught threads of gold in their seams, shimmering softly beneath the light. Music drifted gently through the air, soft enough to invite conversation but thoughtful enough to make silence feel like a choice. These were the nights when champagne flowed, voices lowered, and secrets slipped out between laughs—though some stayed hidden, even from ourselves.

The gala, naturally, was in Manhattan—our city, our stage. The one place that knew how to make a fleeting moment feel permanent. I had flown in from Paris just two days earlier, fresh off a shoot in the Marais. My life was always in motion, and I was always somewhere: London, Milan, Tokyo. But no matter how far I wandered, Manhattan always pulled me back. I missed it more than I admitted. It wasn't just the skyline or the pace. It was the memory of who we were here, the place where we first dared to imagine it all.

I adjusted the sapphire silk draped over my hip and took another sip of champagne—crisp, dry, and expensive enough to matter. My dress embodied understated elegance, hugging every curve with quiet confidence. Beside me, Biljana stood in a striking black sheath, its sleek lines and daring cut mirroring her confidence and quiet strength. She was effortlessly striking, radiating the calm, controlled authority of a powerhouse attorney who regularly topped "40 Under 40" lists without breaking stride. Yet behind her impeccable style and unshakeable courtroom demeanor was someone softer: fiercely loyal, deeply kind, and unfailingly devoted, especially to me.

We were hosting this benefit together. One of many, yes, but this one mattered more. The funds supported an education and housing initiative for refugee girls. Girls who had seen more than they should have. Girls who, in another life, might have been us.

As the applause rose and gently faded, Biljana stepped onto the stage. She didn't need notes. She never did. Her voice was clear, poised, and deliberate.

"There's a photo on the wall over there—girls from Ukraine, Syria, and Sudan. They're holding books, jumping rope, and laughing like girls do when they're allowed to simply be children.

But childhood isn't guaranteed for everyone, is it?

Someone, somewhere, is always deciding who gets to feel safe, who is allowed to remain a child, and who must grow up far too soon.

That's why we're here. Because someone once made a way for us — and now, we make the way for them."

There was a small stillness in the crowd—the kind you don't often get in rooms like this. A moment of admiration and awareness.

I felt it too.

Behind her, one of the posters caught my eye again—a collage of the girls this gala would support. One girl at the edge of the photo had a crooked smile and wild blond curls. Another had eyes that pulled something from the back of my mind—a look I'd seen once in a broken mirror or a worn-out dream. I stared a second longer than I meant to.

Familiar, but impossible. Must've been the lighting. Or the champagne. Yeah... definitely the champagne, I told myself, half-laughing under my breath.

Biljana returned to my side just as a new round of applause swept through. I handed her a second glass.

"Three donors cried," she said with a smirk. "You might break your record."

I clinked my glass to hers. "They cried because you told the truth."

She shrugged. "I always do."

That was our world—a deliberate balance of power and elegance, built on beautiful truths spoken carefully and stitched into the seams of designer gowns. We moved through it with purpose. Every detail curated; every moment intentional. Confidence came naturally, but kindness wasn't optional. We weren't just admired; we were respected. We knew how to hold attention and how to hold back. We made it feel effortless.

And then, of course, there was Miko.

He stood in the corner, shoulder tilted slightly toward the bar, drink in hand, listening to someone half-heartedly. He hadn't changed much—still sharp, still watching more than he spoke. He used to be my agent. We met when I was eighteen, back when I was still learning how to walk into a room without apologizing for taking up space. He was young too then—just a few years older than me and barely getting his footing in the industry. Somehow, we figured it out together.

He once said, "You don't need to be the loudest person in the room, Amanda. Just the one they don't forget."

He wasn't wrong.

We blurred the lines—agent, friend, something more. And then, like all beautiful chaos, it collapsed softly into something else. He and Biljana had grown closer since. I don't ask. I don't need to. At least not yet.

In our world, we didn't fight over love. We let it unfold. We adapted. We moved forward. Always forward. Or at least, that's what I told myself.

I spotted him before he saw us, Miko, in a perfectly cut charcoal suit, his tie casually loose—always more comfortable on the edge of a crowd than in the middle of one. But when his eyes met mine, he smiled like we hadn't lost a single year between then and now.

"Still hiding in corners like a villain in a Bond film," I said as Biljana and I approached.

He raised his glass in salute. "Only the best ones hide in plain sight."

Biljana arched an eyebrow, amused. "He's quoting himself again. It's going to be one of those nights."

Miko grinned. "Come on, you love it."

"I tolerate it," she said, but her eyes softened the way they always did around him—just slightly.

The three of us stood close now, a little triangle of shared history in the glow of a room that was half fantasy, half purpose. For a moment, no one said anything. It was comfortable, mostly. But not weightless.

"I loved your speech," Miko said to Biljana, sincere. "You always know how to thread the needle between heart and power."

She gave a small nod, touched in a way she rarely let show. "It's easy when it's something real."

He turned to me. "And you look..." He took a beat, letting it land, "like you walked straight off a Gaultier dream sequence."

I rolled my eyes, but I smiled. "Just doing my part for the visual storytelling."

We laughed—the way people laugh when they've known each other too well and too long to fake anything.

But underneath the surface, I could feel it. That low hum of knowing. Of memories. Of what used to be mine and now maybe wasn't. Or maybe still was, in some quiet, inconvenient way.

He looked at me a second too long. Or maybe I looked at him.

Biljana broke the silence. "Did you see the poster by the east wall?"

"I did," I said slowly. "One of the girls looked familiar."

"Same here," she replied, her voice suddenly quieter. "I can't place it. But..."

But. Always a but.

Miko tilted his head. "Maybe you both met her at one of the other fundraisers."

"Maybe," I said, though something in my chest resisted that explanation. "Or maybe we're just getting too used to remembering."

Another pause.

Then Miko touched his glass gently to mine. "To remembering the right things."

And Biljana added, "And to forgetting the ones that tried to bury us."

It landed between us like an unspoken truth—too distant to define, too familiar to ignore.

We clinked glasses and drank.

And in that candlelit space, beneath the glitter and speeches and elegant poses, I wondered, not for the first time, how long you can live inside a dream before it starts to remember who you really are.

Chapter Two

CHAPTER TWO

The ride home was quiet, but comfortable—like sitting with someone who just knows you. Biljana and I had been best friends since we were kids—the kind of friends who grew up side by side through every awkward phase and big life change. Maybe it was because everything around us felt so uncertain. We had families, yes, but family was complicated, so we clung to each other instead. Maybe that's what made it different from friendship. It was something quieter. Older. Woven into the fabric of who we were.

We were a long way from those childhood days, yet our lives had a way of folding back into each other, even when we didn't plan it. That's what kept us close. We weren't just friends; we were each other's constants, confidants, and the only family within reach. More than anyone else, it was each other we held on to. We'd grown up modestly, side by side, then moved away and dared to build something bigger. That shared grit shaped us—made us resilient, confident, and quietly kind. We'd made a promise, even if unspoken: to give back what we once needed, to protect others the way no one had protected us. And maybe, most of all, to never let anyone diminish the lives we'd fought to build.

Across from me, Biljana swirled her champagne and tilted her head back, letting out a slow breath as the city lights flickered across her cheekbones.

"We did good tonight," she said finally. "They were listening."

I nodded, lifting my own glass in a soft toast. "To little girls with big dreams."

Then—quiet. The kind that says more than it hides. I leaned back, letting the silence settle between us until she broke it.

"I couldn't stop staring at that one poster," she said, softer now. "The girl in the red scarf."

My brow furrowed. "I know. I saw her too. And another one. I had this weird... feeling."

Biljana nodded. "Like we'd seen them before."

"Yeah," I whispered. "But not here. Somewhere else." I didn't say more, and neither did she.

The silence that followed wasn't heavy. Just uncertain.

She cleared her throat and shifted gears, as if on instinct. "Miko looked sharp tonight."

I rolled my eyes, just enough to make her smirk. "Don't pivot this on me. You're the one doing dinner twice a week with him."

"Oh, come on," she laughed, brushing a stray hair from her face. "You're the one who brought him into our world."

"I was eighteen," I said. "He told me I could light up runways in Milan, and I believed him."

"He wasn't wrong."

"Still... things ended messy between us. Business got tangled with... everything else."

Biljana studied me for a moment, then I asked quietly, "You and Miko... what is it, really?"

Her smile faded, replaced by something more complicated. "I don't know. Easy? Familiar?"

"Dangerous?" I offered.

She laughed again, but it didn't last. "It won't come between us, you know."

"I know," I said quickly. "But it's hard pretending it doesn't feel strange."

She gave me that look—the one that always made me feel ten again, hiding under the blankets with a flashlight and a stack of catalogs, imagining who we'd grow up to be.

In the back of the car, the city slipped past in blurs of light. We sat in that easy, wordless quiet—the kind that says more than conversation ever could—both of us lost in thoughts we didn't yet dare to share.

When the car dropped me at my building, I watched her step into the lobby next door before I took the elevator to my own penthouse. We liked our space—we needed it, even—but the truth was, we'd always lived close. As if proximity were a shield. As if we'd fall apart without the other nearby.

Back at my place, the weight of the night settled over me—the kind that makes you want to peel off the evening piece by piece. I slipped off my heels, poured a half-glass of champagne, and wandered to the window. The city at night always had a way of holding me still, its lights sparking little moments of reflection. Tonight, it buzzed below, lit up and untouchable, like it belonged to a version of me I hadn't been in a while.

I took a slow sip, letting my gaze drift back into the room until it caught on the shelf beside the glass—lined with books and small keepsakes, the kind of clutter that carried stories.

I smiled when I spotted the photo album. I hadn't looked at it in years, but something about tonight made me want to flip through real memories—ones you could actually hold in your hands.

I pulled it from the shelf and sank into the armchair, letting the album rest in my lap. Tonight, more than ever, I needed something real—something to ground me in a version of the past that still felt like mine.

The cover creaked open easily, the pages flipping back to sun-faded snapshots of Biljana and me: gap-toothed grins, messy ponytails, plastic sunglasses we wore like they were designer. The kind of childhood moments that made you laugh and ache all at once.

I turned another page, and there he was. Miko's young, smiling face stared back at me, frozen in a moment of unguarded laughter, his arm draped casually around my shoulders. His eyes were locked on mine with an intensity I'd always noticed but rarely acknowledged aloud. It was a look of genuine care, shaded with something deeper. Something romantic.

I traced the edge of the photo with my fingertip. Our history had always danced somewhere between professionalism and something more—a blur of late-night planning sessions, laughter spilling into dawn, whispered conversations just inches apart, and moments when boundaries disappeared entirely. But we never defined it. Never openly acknowledged what we both clearly felt. And now, looking back, I wondered what we'd lost. What we might have been. If anything remained of those hidden feelings I'd so carefully tucked away.

Maybe there had always been something deeper, hidden behind our polished facades. Something I'd secretly hoped might one day surface, only to watch it quietly drift into Biljana's world instead. A sigh slipped out—heavier than I expected.

I started flipping faster, as if speed could outrun the unease creeping in. I wasn't ready to see Miko's face again, so I searched for anything else—anyone else.

Page after page blurred by, until one made me pause.

At first, it looked fine—familiar, ordinary. But then, the edges seemed to shift, just slightly. Like the moment you realize something's out of place, but can't quite name what.

And there it was. A flash of red.

My chest tightened. That scarf. That flicker of something I couldn't explain.

It was a photo of me, standing next to a girl I didn't recognize.

She was smiling. Calm. Effortless.

And around her neck was a red scarf.

I froze.

The color hit me like a siren—too bold to ignore, too familiar to make sense. My eyes narrowed. Her face... there was something about it. Not quite recognizable, but not entirely unknown either. Like a word stuck on the tip of your tongue.

Wait. That's it.

She looked just like the girl from the poster at the benefit gala.

But how could that be?

My pulse quickened.

I flipped the album back a few pages, then forward again. Same photo. Same girl. Same scarf.

Why didn't I remember this moment? This person?

And why did I feel like I should?

Was it the champagne? Fatigue? Stress?

Or was something I'd buried finally pushing its way to the surface?

"I just need a second," I murmured, gripping the edges of the album tighter than I meant to.

The champagne glass in my other hand wobbled, nearly tipping before I caught it without looking. I set it down, suddenly unsure if I'd even taken a sip.

I blinked. Hard. Once. Twice. The room felt slightly off-kilter, like the lighting had shifted a few degrees off center.

The photo under my fingers didn't feel like paper anymore. It was slick, almost fluid—colors bleeding, edges softening, as if the memory itself was resisting definition.

My limbs grew heavy. Not tired, just... slowed. Like the night was sinking into me. I wanted to stay with the feeling, chase it, pin it down. But it was already slipping.

The album slid from my hands and landed with a soft thud on the floor.

I leaned back into the cushion, eyes half-closed, watching the room dissolve into shadows and light.

Everything blurred until it no longer mattered what was real.

Chapter Three

CHAPTER THREE

S unlight poured through the windows as I sat up, wincing at the tight pull in my neck. On the rug, the scattered photographs caught the soft morning light—glossy, familiar snapshots of childhood, college days, Miko. Real memories. I exhaled slowly, a wave of relief washing over me. The champagne, the gala—it had all blurred into a strange, unsettling dream, and nothing more. Probably.

Coffee, I told myself. First coffee, then water. But the mess on the floor held me in place. I bent to gather the photos, but my fingers brushed something soft tucked beneath the album—a ribbon, deep red, the kind that might once have wrapped a gift. I held it in my hands, turning it over as if it should mean something, should unlock a memory just out of reach. Nothing came. Just silence—the same blankness that followed me from last night. With a sigh, I set it aside. Maybe that was why the scarf had found me in my dreams.

The morning felt brighter now, clearer, even if the unease lingered quietly in the back of my mind. I made my way to the kitchen and brewed a strong cup of coffee—black, no sugar, with a splash of cream, just the way I liked it. The steam curled upward, warm and grounding. Exactly what I needed.

After coffee, I slipped into my morning routine. The shower came next, hot water easing the ache in my neck and, for the first time since last night, leaving my mind blissfully blank. No nagging thoughts. No flickers of half-remembered images. Just silence. I smiled, letting the moment wash over me, as if it could rinse everything away—the gala, the dream, the uneasy questions. It felt good. It felt right.

By the time I unrolled my yoga mat by the window, I almost felt like myself again. Breathe in. Stretch. Exhale. My body found its rhythm easily, but my mind drifted back to the red scarf. Why did it feel so familiar? I pushed the thought aside. Not now. Not again.

When my mind spun like this—loud, unsettled, too sharp at the edges—I always reached for control. Anxiety needed anchors, and mine had always been flowers. Pulling them from the fridge, lining them up stem by stem, I could finally breathe. It was simple, almost meditative: order, symmetry, beauty I could create with my own hands.

The leftovers from the gala waited—white calla lilies, soft pink peonies, and one bold red rose. For a moment, it felt off. A detail out of place in a room I knew by heart. I let the thought pass. What I needed now was the ritual—the steadiness of stems and water, the quiet kind of control I could hold.

It wasn't just the arranging. It was the memory. Back home in Europe, Mom always kept fresh flowers on the table. No matter how hard life got, there was always something alive, something beautiful in the middle of it. Maybe that's why the ritual stayed with me. It wasn't just about flowers; it was about hope.

My phone rang, breaking the quiet.

"Hey, it's Biljana." Her voice was warm, but a little hesitant.

"Hey," I said, smiling.

"I'm grabbing dinner with Miko tonight. You want to come?"

I hesitated. "Is this really about dinner, or is it more about last night's conversation?"

She laughed softly. "Maybe a little of both."

"I'm flying out early for a shoot in Milan tomorrow," I said quickly, tucking a stray petal behind my ear. "Can't really do dinner tonight."

There was a pause. "Okay. I get it."

I knew what she meant. This wasn't just a casual dinner invite; it was the start of something new for them. And maybe the end of something unspoken for me. I wasn't ready to face that. I wasn't ready to let go of the quiet illusion that Miko still belonged to me in some way, even if we hadn't been us in a long time.

"Have a good night," I said.

"You too. Travel safe."

I ended the call, feeling that familiar mix of warmth and distance that defined us—always close, yet with unspoken things lingering just beneath the surface.

Packing seemed like the most logical distraction. Neat piles of carefully chosen outfits, a toiletry bag zipped with precision, chargers, and passport in their designated spots. Efficient. Detached. Safe.

But the silence of the apartment grew too loud. So I slipped on my coat and decided to walk. Just a few blocks. Just enough to breathe in the cool air and feel something other than the weight pressing behind my eyes.

I didn't plan the route. My feet just took me there, like a familiar song playing in my head.

The little restaurant on the corner with the green awning and copper lanterns. The one Miko and I used to duck into for working lunches and late-night strategy sessions that blurred into laughter and second glasses of wine. Back when we made sense.

I paused at the window, my breath catching before I even saw them.

There they were.

Biljana and Miko—seated at the corner table by the window, leaning in like the rest of the world had disappeared. Smiling in that soft, tentative way that meant something new was beginning. Her hand rested near his on the table. His eyes didn't leave hers.

And then... the kiss.

It wasn't dramatic. It wasn't showy. It was delicate. Familiar. Like they'd done it a thousand times in their minds before finally letting it happen.

My heart sank. Not from jealousy, but from the ache of inevitability. The sharp pull of knowing I was watching something beautiful that no longer belonged to me.

I looked away. Quickly. Too quickly. And kept walking, like the cold might numb what I already knew.

Chapter Four

CHAPTER FOUR

The Milan shoot had come and gone—flashes, fittings, interviews, applause. I smiled on cue and wore every dress like it was armor, but my mind had been somewhere else the entire time. Somewhere back home. Somewhere across a restaurant window.

Now, three days later, I was back in New York, curled on the sofa with a cashmere throw, a cup of tea growing cold in my hand. The rain had started just after I landed and hadn't let up since—soft, steady, oddly comforting.

I hadn't seen Biljana since the call. We texted—nothing heavy. Updates, questions, emojis. But I'd been dodging the inevitable. Until now.

The knock was soft, but she didn't wait for me to answer. The door opened with a quiet click—her key, of course. We were still each other's emergency contact. Still friends in all the ways that mattered, even if everything felt a little sideways now.

I didn't move from the couch.

Biljana stepped in slowly, closing the door behind her like she wasn't sure she belonged here. Her coat was damp at the shoulders, rain clinging to her curls.

"You're home," she said, setting her umbrella in the stand by the door. "I figured... I mean, I hoped."

I nodded and offered a tired smile. "Jet lag makes terrible company."

She crossed the room without asking, pausing just long enough to glance at the untouched tea in my hands before settling on the edge of the armchair.

For a moment, we just sat there—rain threading down the windows, the clock ticking somewhere in the background. The kind of silence that meant something was coming.

"I've been meaning to come by," she said finally, her voice low. "But I wasn't sure if you'd want me to."

"I saw you," I said—not cruelly, not dramatically. Just the truth, laid bare between us. "At the restaurant. The night before I left."

Her breath caught. "You did?"

"I was just walking by," I said. "Didn't plan it. I didn't even go in. I just... saw."

She closed her eyes for a moment, the weight of that settling in.

"You looked happy," I added, though it tasted strange in my mouth. Not bitter. Just unfamiliar.

Biljana shifted. "It wasn't planned, Amanda. That kiss. I mean... we didn't go into that dinner thinking—"

"I know," I interrupted gently. "You don't have to explain."

But she did. And I needed her to.

"I think I've been trying not to want him," she said, fingers tangling in the fringe of the throw pillow. "Out of loyalty to you. Out of fear that it would wreck this—us."

I swallowed hard. "It doesn't wreck us."

We both knew that wasn't entirely true. Not yet. But saying it out loud gave the idea a place to breathe.

A beat passed. Then another.

"You know what the strangest part is?" I said. "I wasn't even angry. I was... I don't know. Disoriented. Like I was watching something shift in real time. Like I stepped into the future without warning."

She gave a soft, sad smile. "That's exactly how it feels."

I finally set my tea down, letting the warmth fade from my palms. "You're not asking for permission. And I'm not giving it. But I do want to understand."

Biljana looked up. "And I want to be careful with you."

That, at least, was something we could hold onto. Something that still felt real.

We sat like that for a while—me in my cocoon of soft knits, her with rain in her hair, both of us balancing on the edge of something new.

Eventually, Biljana let out a breath and leaned back. "You know what we haven't even talked about?"

I raised an eyebrow.

"The party," she said. "It's almost December, and we haven't planned a thing."

I let out a dry laugh. "God, you're right. The New Year's Eve party."

It had always been our thing—decadent themes, guest lists longer than we remembered writing, towers of champagne, chaos, glamour, glitter. And somehow, it always worked.

"I guess we should figure it out," I said. "Even if everything else feels a little... different this year."

Biljana grinned. "Different isn't always bad."

I looked at her. Really looked at her. And maybe, just maybe, I believed her.

"Alright then," I said, pushing the throw aside. "Let's plan something unforgettable."

Thunder cracked in the distance, low and mean.

We both flinched.

The rain, which had been falling gently all afternoon, suddenly turned frantic—slamming against the windows with sharp gusts of wind.

I stood and walked to the window. "That came out of nowhere."

Biljana joined me, peering into the smeared blur of city lights. "They said rain, but not this."

Then the lights flickered.

We both froze.

A half-second later, everything cut out—lights, heater, the quiet hum of the fridge. Darkness swelled around us like a second skin.

Everything inside me pulled tight. My body moved before my brain caught up, and Biljana moved too—fast, like muscle memory. We met in the hallway at the same moment, eyes wide in the sudden dark.

"Oh, wait," I muttered. "Flashlight—hang on."

I stumbled into the closet, grabbed it from the top shelf, and clicked it on. The weak beam bounced, caught her face, then mine in the hallway mirror. Both of us pale. Too pale.

We stood still for a moment, like statues under glass. The silence had a weight to it—thick and familiar, as if it had been waiting for us to notice.

My muscles ached from staying so still. I shifted—just slightly—and my foot hit the umbrella stand.

"Dang it!" I hissed, catching myself against the wall. The flashlight slipped from my hand and skittered across the hardwood in a slow, spiraling roll of yellow light.

A laugh burst out of me before I could stop it—sharp, startled, and wrong. Biljana looked at me, and for a second, we both just stared, unsure if we were laughing or on the edge of tears.

Biljana blinked. "Are you okay?"

"Yeah," I said, still half-laughing, half-panting. "That was... a little much."

She smiled, but her voice was thin. "We both overreacted."

"Yeah," I said. "We really did."

We stood there, the flashlight casting strange shadows across the ceiling, the storm raging beyond the windows.

The silence felt too loud. Like an old song we both recognized but couldn't quite name.

Biljana cleared her throat. "That was weird, right?"

I nodded slowly. "Yeah. Weird."

Neither of us said anything more.

I picked up the flashlight, and we walked back to the couch.

Outside, the wind howled down the street, tugging at tree branches and traffic lights like something trying to get in.

Inside, we sat in the dark, waiting for the lights to come back on.

But I couldn't shake the feeling that something else had just flickered to life.

Chapter Five

CHAPTER FIVE

The power came back around 3 a.m. Neither of us had moved. We'd fallen asleep on opposite ends of the couch, the flashlight dim between us, casting a faint golden beam across the coffee table like a forgotten lighthouse.

By morning, the storm was gone. Outside, the city was washed clean—sharp and bright. But inside, something still felt off-kilter. Like the air hadn't reset along with the power.

Biljana made coffee while I stared blankly at a bowl of grapefruit I never touched. We didn't talk about the night before—no mention of how we'd both bolted at the same time, or how the dark had hit us like a memory we didn't have words for. We pretended we'd overreacted. That it was funny. A moment. Nothing more.

By late afternoon, she left with a tight hug and a promise to meet later in the week to go over venue options.

I told her I'd send notes.

I didn't.

I spent the next day trying to get back to normal—the kind that makes you feel like you're still in control.

Hair appointment. Facial. A wardrobe pull for an upcoming shoot in Tribeca. I kept my head down, smiled politely, and made lists I never looked at again.

I needed something small to fix. Something that could be arranged, decided, and contained.

Flowers were always my lane. Every party, every shoot, every holiday—we had an unspoken system. Biljana handled vendors and timelines. I handled aesthetics and florals. It was the one task that felt more like instinct than obligation. So I walked to the florist, notebook in hand, pretending I was just doing my part.

The air inside was thick with eucalyptus and roses—sharp and sweet. Vases lined the walls like little altars, waiting to be filled. I gave the girl at the front my name, and she disappeared into the back to retrieve the sample order.

While I waited, I drifted toward the worktable by the window, where an older woman was assembling small bundles of carnations and white freesia. Her hands moved slowly but precisely. Graceful, like she'd done it for decades.

She looked up at me and smiled. Warm. Knowing.

"You always preferred the lilies," she said.

I blinked.

The air stilled, just slightly.

"I'm sorry?" I asked, studying her face.

She tilted her head. "Oh. Forgive me—I must've mistaken you for someone else." A pause. "You just reminded me of a girl I used to know. From a long time ago."

I forced a polite smile, suddenly unsure of my footing.

The assistant returned with the sample bundle, and I paid quickly, the stems trembling slightly in my hand as I stepped back into the crisp air outside.

The air felt sharper, colder. I kept replaying her tone in my head—not the words, but the certainty in them, like she knew something I had forgotten.

I walked home slower than usual, hugging the flowers close to my chest like they might anchor me. The woman's voice echoed in my mind.

You always preferred the lilies.

It shouldn't have meant anything. Probably didn't. But it lingered longer than it should have, like a thread tugging at something I hadn't realized was loose.

Back upstairs, I set the bouquet in the sink and stood still, watching the water fill the vase. The lilies opened slightly as the stems drank, tilting their pale faces toward the light. There was something solemn about them today—too still, too knowing.

I shook it off and poured a glass of wine. The couch still held the shape of Biljana's body from the night before.

I should have texted her. Told her the storm left a strange feeling in the air. Told her about the florist. But instead, I opened my notebook and stared at the blank page.

Nothing came—just the kind of stillness that makes you think too much.

I closed my eyes and let the sound of the city drift through the window—the distant hum of traffic, the hush of tires on wet pavement, a faint car horn somewhere uptown.

Then, without thinking, I reached for my phone and saw a missed call from Miko. My pulse quickened.

Miko? Why would he call me now?

A wave of dread swept over me—heavy and sudden. I wasn't ready for whatever conversation he wanted. Wasn't ready to revisit us. Not tonight. Not yet.

But before I could put the phone down, it buzzed again, louder this time—a text lighting up the screen:

Miko:

Sorry for the late notice, but we need you for a shoot tomorrow. You're the only one who can pull this off. Call me?

My heart skipped, curiosity and anxiety twisting together. Working closely with Miko again—now, of all times—felt dangerous.

But it was work, wasn't it? Just work.

I hesitated, thumb hovering over his name, knowing I had no real choice at all.

Chapter Six

CHAPTER SIX

I pressed the phone to my ear, heart pounding despite my attempt to sound calm. "Hey, Miko. What's going on?"

There was a beat of silence—just long enough to signal hesitation. "Amanda. Hey." His voice was smooth, casual, effortlessly polished like always. Too casual.

"Late call," I said, trying to match his tone. "Must be important."

He laughed lightly, as though trying to diffuse something unspoken. "You know me, always last-minute. Listen, it's a big shoot tomorrow. They specifically asked for you."

I raised an eyebrow, even though he couldn't see it. "You're not even my agent anymore, Miko. Seems odd they'd go through you to book me."

Another pause, shorter this time but still noticeable. "Well, they trust me, and I trust you. Seemed like a natural fit."

I sighed, leaning back against the counter. My patience thinned, my tone sharpened. "Are we really doing this?"

"Doing what?" he asked, innocence thinly veiled in his voice.

"Pretending there's no other reason you're calling me," I shot back, the edge of frustration cutting through. "I don't need charity work, Miko. Or guilt jobs."

He sighed audibly, the façade slipping slightly. "Amanda, it's not charity, and it's definitely not guilt. I just—"

"You just what?" I interrupted softly, my voice betraying more vulnerability than I'd intended. "Need to know we're still okay, despite whatever's happening with Biljana?"

Another silence, heavier this time. Finally, he spoke quietly, sincerity breaking through the practiced charm. "I guess, yeah. Is that wrong?"

I closed my eyes, suddenly weary. "No, it's not wrong. But you could've just asked."

His tone shifted, more open, more real. "Then I'm asking now. Are we okay?"

I hesitated, took a breath, and steadied my voice. "We'll find out tomorrow, won't we?"

He let out a small, relieved laugh. "Fair enough. I'll text you the details, and I'll see you there."

"See you there," I echoed softly, ending the call before my voice gave away anything else.

The next morning was a blur of urgency—wardrobe fittings, rushed makeup, last-minute adjustments. It all felt surreal, yet somehow familiar—the kind of rhythm that usually steadied me, but today felt just a beat behind.

The shoot was at a sunlit studio downtown, an airy space with white walls and floor-to-ceiling windows overlooking the city. Assistants moved around me in practiced rhythm, the hum of blow-dryers and soft laughter filling the air. Powder drifted through the sunlight as the makeup artist spoke, her words soft and steady, but they reached me as if from another room.

Beneath the shimmer and precision, something inside me felt slightly askew, as if the surface of things had shifted and I was pretending not to see it.

When I finally stepped onto the set, adjusting the delicate fabric of my gown, I caught sight of Miko standing in the corner, eyes intent on the setup. He looked effortlessly comfortable, engaged in a quiet conversation with the creative director. Something in my chest tightened at how easily he fit into this space, into this world—a world we'd once shared.

He turned suddenly, eyes meeting mine across the busy room. His expression softened, warmth flickering behind his professional composure. He walked over, hands tucked casually in his pockets, his gaze never leaving mine.

As I stepped onto the set, adjusting the neckline of my gown, Miko caught sight of me from across the room. His posture straightened slightly, eyes following my every movement with a familiarity that felt too close and too far all at once.

He waited until I neared the edge of the set, then approached, his expression unreadable but softer than I expected.

"Thanks for doing this," he said, his voice low, almost hesitant. "I knew you'd be the perfect fit. This kind of shoot... it needs someone who understands elegance like it's second nature."

I searched his face for subtext, but it gave nothing away. Still, the way he said elegance—like it meant more than clothes and cameras—made something shift in me.

"Of course," I replied, trying to match his tone, though my smile wavered at the edges. "It's what I do."

We moved around each other with quiet choreography, staying just outside each other's reach. He wasn't adjusting my poses or calling out cues like he once did—but he watched, always watched, and when our eyes met between takes, it was like flipping through old pages of a book neither of us had finished.

There was admiration in his gaze, but also distance. Regret, maybe. Or recognition of something lost. Each passing moment felt like walking a tightrope between past and present, between what might have been and what never was.

Afterward, we found ourselves sitting quietly in his car outside the studio, the city around us humming gently as daylight waned into evening. I stared out the window, tracing invisible patterns on the glass.

"Amanda," he began, voice careful, "are you really okay?"

I hesitated, the immediate reassurance sticking unspoken in my throat. Instead, I found myself admitting quietly, "It just feels strange—us working together again, pretending everything's simple. It's like stepping into an old version of myself, but she's not quite there anymore."

Miko considered this, his gaze distant but thoughtful. "We both changed," he admitted softly. "But maybe who we were back then still matters. Maybe that connection we had isn't something you can just erase, even if things change."

"I don't know," I whispered, my voice barely audible. "Sometimes I think about who we might've been if we'd allowed ourselves to define what we were. I wonder if things would've turned out differently."

He sighed deeply, eyes briefly closing. "I wonder that too. More often than you think." He paused, a vulnerability I'd rarely heard from him slipping into his voice. "I miss what we had, Amanda.

The simplicity. The way we understood each other without words. Sometimes I wish we could just... go back."

My heart fluttered, a familiar ache settling deep within. The air between us thickened, and for a moment, I felt an undeniable pull toward him. My gaze dropped to his lips, memories flooding back, warmth spreading through me. The desire to lean in, to close the small distance between us, was overwhelming—but I held back, anchored by reality.

"I know," I finally breathed, voice trembling slightly. "But we can't. Not anymore."

His expression softened further, understanding clouding his eyes as he nodded slowly. "I know. It's different now." He reached out hesitantly, gently brushing a strand of hair behind my ear, the contact brief but charged. "But I'm glad we had today."

"Me, too," I whispered, pulling back gently. Silence fell again, but it was comfortable this time, each of us processing our own thoughts, holding onto this fleeting moment of honesty.

"I should go," I murmured softly, breaking the stillness. He nodded silently, eyes gentle, still holding all those things we hadn't said, wouldn't say now.

I stepped out of the car and closed the door behind me, feeling the faint chill of the evening air replace the warmth we'd briefly created.

"We'll be okay. I just need a moment to breathe and process."

Back in my apartment, a gentle sadness settled over me—for everything we'd never be—but beneath it stirred a quiet clarity: a sense of finally being ready to move forward.

With a deep, deliberate breath, I pushed off the door and made my way to the kitchen, pulling a bottle of wine from the fridge. I poured a generous glass—tonight, I deserved at least that—and retrieved the pint of ice cream tucked away in the freezer for moments exactly like these.

Settling onto the couch, legs curled beneath me, I dug the spoon deep into creamy, indulgent vanilla swirled with caramel and chocolate.

It felt cliché, but there was comfort in that predictability.

This was how you moved forward—one spoonful of ice cream, one sip of wine at a time.

Halfway through, I glanced at my phone, a reflex kicking in. Normally, this was the exact moment I'd call Biljana—the one person who would understand instantly, who'd come rushing over with more wine, her sharp wit, and endless comfort. But tonight... tonight was different. Tonight, calling her wasn't an option—not with Miko standing squarely between us. The realization stung with surprising sharpness.

I let out a soft laugh, shaking my head at the irony of it all. Here I was, heart aching because of a man who had become the wedge between the one person I'd always leaned on to mend exactly this kind of heartache and me. It was almost comical.

A sigh slipped out, quieter this time, carrying with it a faint sense of release. Tomorrow, I thought, would be different. Tomorrow, I could find the resolve to let go, move forward, and create space for something new. But tonight—tonight was for feeling, for quiet self-pity, and the uncomplicated solace of wine and ice cream.

And maybe, I decided with another remorseful laugh, that was okay.

Sometime after the fourth glass—though if I was honest, it was probably closer to an entire bottle—I found myself crawling into bed. No shower, no pajamas, just me, sinking into cool sheets, feeling strangely liberated by abandoning my nightly rituals. I simply didn't have the energy or heart for routine tonight.

All I wanted was sleep—deep, uncomplicated sleep—to cleanse my mind, reset my heart, and let me wake up tomorrow without thoughts of Miko lingering around the edges of my consciousness.

Yes, tomorrow. Tomorrow would be my fresh start, a clean slate.

At least, that's what I whispered softly to myself as I closed my eyes, letting the comforting darkness pull me gently under.

Chapter Seven

CHAPTER SEVEN

The café was buzzing when I arrived, a quiet hum of polished chaos—phones buzzing, spoons clinking, people performing the ease of everyday life. Biljana spotted me through the glass and waved, her bracelets catching the light. When I stepped inside, she rose from her chair, and we met halfway for a quick hug that lingered just a second longer than casual. She smelled faintly of jasmine and espresso.

I slipped into the seat across from her, watching as she smoothed her coat sleeve and lifted her cup again. She looked every bit like someone untouched by sleepless nights, composed in that effortless way that always drew eyes. I envied how she could make exhaustion look elegant. I'd always admired that about her. No matter the hour or the chaos, Biljana always looked composed—spectacular, even. She had a way of commanding a room without demanding it, whether it was the courtroom or a café.

This one, our café, had been our refuge for years—the little French bakery and café on the corner called Le Chalet. We stumbled upon it ages ago, back when we were still finding our footing in this city, before the world started calling our names. Back then, it felt like a luxury we could barely afford: the glossy pastries behind glass, the cappuccinos topped with perfect foam, the sense that important people came here to be seen. Somewhere along the way, it stopped being a splurge and became a ritual—the place where we planned parties, galas, and entire seasons of our lives.

The next hour slipped by in a familiar rhythm, planning the kind of details that make an evening unforgettable. The décor, the atmosphere, the music, and champagne. The food, the desserts, and of course, our signature fireworks show—the real showstopper of the night.

The guest list came last, as it always did. The usual circle first, then close friends, then the names that made the room feel important—local celebrities, art patrons, the city's well-dressed benefactors. We didn't invite them for their charm; we invited them for what their presence meant. I didn't always agree that these people belonged at our private celebrations, but New Year's was different. Everyone wanted to be at the party that night—and when you needed generosity later, it helped if they remembered who hosted the best one.

As the planning wound down, our conversation drifted into the familiar—work updates, travel plans, the small details that fill the spaces between big moments. I could sense she wanted to bring up Miko, but hesitation lingered in her eyes. She didn't want to cross that line. Not yet.

But it was time. Time for me to let go and fall into something new—for them, and for myself.

I leaned into the quiet resolve that had been forming over the last few days, the slow unwinding of something that had lived too long in the in-between. Miko hadn't been mine for a long time. Maybe he never truly was. What we shared—or almost shared—existed in its own small, beautiful season of my life, and that was enough.

Now, it was time to release the what-ifs, the maybes, the unfinished edges. To make space for something fresh, something untangled. A new beginning for them—and a new chapter for me.

Still, a small ache pulsed beneath the acceptance. I realized it wasn't just about love, or the memory of it. It was about friendship—the ease of knowing he'd always be there when I needed steadiness. Maybe that was what I feared losing most.

But perhaps not.

The three of us had always moved like constellations—separate but connected, never losing our orbit.

Biljana had always been more than a friend. She was my sister in every way that mattered—the one who'd weathered every storm with me. And that, I decided, I could never lose.

So if my heart had to make room for her and Miko together, it would—as long as it didn't have to lose her.

"Biljana," I began softly, her name landing gently in the space between us, heavier than it should've been. She met my gaze, eyes searching mine, as if she already knew what was coming.

"I know things have been... different lately," I said carefully. "Between you and Miko, I mean."

A flicker crossed her face—the faintest tremor of emotion beneath her polished calm. "Amanda, I—"

I shook my head gently before she could finish. "You don't have to explain. Really. I think I've known for a while. Maybe I just wasn't ready to say it out loud."

Her composure cracked, barely. She looked down at her cup, tracing the rim with her finger. When she finally spoke, her voice was softer than I'd ever heard it.

"I didn't want to hurt you. You're my best friend. You're..." Her words caught. "You're like a sister I always wanted."

Something inside me ached at that—not from pain, but from the weight of the bond that had survived everything else.

"I know," I said. "And you haven't hurt me. Not really. I just needed to sit with it long enough to understand what it meant, and what it didn't. That some things aren't meant to be kept. Only remembered."

Biljana looked up again, and there it was—vulnerability, pure and unguarded. "It's not simple with him," she admitted, shaking her head slightly. "It never was. But when I'm with him... it feels easy. And that scares me."

Her honesty disarmed me. "Maybe that's how you know it's real," I said softly.

We sat in silence for a few beats—the kind that only exists between two people who've already said everything that matters.

Then I drew in a steady breath. "Both of you. Whatever this becomes—or doesn't become—I'm okay. Truly. What Miko and I had was... something unfinished, but long ago. A maybe that was never meant to last. But you—" I paused, smiling faintly. "You're my person. You always have been. I'd never want to stand in the way of that."

Biljana's eyes shimmered. She reached across the table, taking my hand with a tenderness that felt like apology and gratitude all at once. "You're sure?" she asked, her voice breaking the tiniest bit.

"I'm sure," I said, squeezing her hand back. "Life's too short for what-ifs."

We drifted into lighter talk once the heavier things had settled—stories from old shoots, gossip about designers, the kind of laughter that felt easy again. The sound of it filled our little corner, soft and genuine, like an exhale we didn't know we'd been holding.

I reached for my bag, ready to settle the check, when the door chimed behind us.

A familiar voice broke through the hum of conversation.

"Well, if it isn't my favorite power duo."

Biljana and I both turned.

"Laura!" Biljana exclaimed, her face lighting up.

There she was—her cousin, wrapped in a camel coat and that effortless Brooklyn-meets-boardroom style only Laura could pull off.

She grinned, already making her way to our table. "I was sure that was you two. Still plotting the next big event?"

"Always," Biljana laughed. "Come, join us—we're planning the New Year's gala. You're invited, of course."

"Of course I am," Laura said, sliding into the seat beside me, shaking the snow from her scarf. "Wouldn't miss the best party in the city."

Her smile was bright, but something in it—some half-formed memory—made the air feel charged, expectant, as though a door had just opened somewhere I couldn't see.

Chapter Eight

CHAPTER EIGHT

Laura loosened her scarf and set her bag beside the chair, brushing the last of the snow from her coat. "So," she said with a grin, "the Ritz again this year? You two really don't know how to do simple, do you?"

Biljana laughed. "We tried once. It didn't suit us."

Laura smiled, shaking her head. "Speaking of the Ritz—do you remember when we were little and used to pretend we were going to parties there?"

She leaned back, eyes bright with amusement. "You wore that long, silky red scarf like it was a gown, and we made invitations out of notebook paper. I was the coat-check girl, remember?"

I blinked. "The red scarf?"

Laura nodded. "Yes! You tied it around your shoulders and said it made you feel elegant." She laughed softly, lost for a moment in her own memory. "You both looked so serious, practicing how to walk in heels that didn't fit."

Biljana smiled politely, but her eyes flickered toward mine. "You're sure that was us?" she asked lightly. "That doesn't sound like something I'd forget."

Laura looked between us, suddenly uncertain. "Of course, it was. I remember it so clearly."

The air at the table shifted—just slightly, but enough for me to feel it. I managed a small laugh, trying to smooth the moment. "Maybe you're thinking of someone else," I offered.

"Maybe," Laura said, though her voice carried doubt. Then, brightening again, she added, "Either way, it's funny how those little games turn into real life sometimes, isn't it?"

She reached for her cup, the conversation spilling forward easily, but my thoughts stayed behind.

The red scarf—again. What is it about red scarves and my memory?

The pretend parties at the Ritz? I don't remember ever imagining the Ritz. It shouldn't have meant anything.

And yet the thought lingered, sharp and quiet—the uneasy sense that maybe I didn't forget at all.

Maybe I'd buried it. And maybe there was a reason I didn't want to remember.

A faint chill crept over me—not from fear exactly, but from the sudden awareness that forgetting and remembering might not be opposites after all— just two sides of the same fracture.

Laura's phone buzzed on the table, snapping her out of the memory.

"Ah—work. I have to run," she said, standing quickly and looping the scarf back around her neck. "Don't forget to send me the invite. I'll see you both soon."

Biljana stood to hug her. "You'll get it delivered this week," she said with a grin. "Scented and hand-delivered, of course—you know we can't do anything halfway."

Laura laughed. "Wouldn't expect anything less."

I rose too, leaning in to hug her. "It was so good seeing you, Laura. It's been too long."

"Far too long," she said warmly, squeezing my hand before turning to leave.

The door chimed behind her as she stepped out, her driver already waiting at the curb.

Biljana sank back into her seat, exhaling a quiet laugh. "She always did have a wild imagination. The Ritz? Red scarves? None of that rings a bell."

"Yeah," I said slowly, stirring the last of my coffee, though it had gone cold. "She must've mixed us up with someone else."

But even as I said it, the words felt thin—rehearsed.

The echo of that red scarf clung to me, like a thread I couldn't see but somehow felt tightening between my ribs.

Biljana glanced at her watch and began gathering her things. "Let's meet at the venue tomorrow, go over the layout before the fireworks team arrives?"

"Sure," I said, my voice steady again. "Tomorrow."

We stood, hugged goodbye, and stepped out into the fading light.

The city was caught in that soft, in-between hour—where shadows lengthened, and the sky hovered between silver and gold.

Snow drifted quietly around us as we paused on the sidewalk, adjusting coats and scarves before heading in opposite directions. I hesitated, something flickering at the edge of my thoughts.

"Oh—before I forget," I said, pulling out my phone. "Did you get the invite for Valérie Duval's new show tomorrow? The one called *Love Affair*?"

Biljana frowned and tapped into her messages.

"Hmm... I don't think—oh." Her face lit up. "Here it is. I must've completely missed it."

"It looks incredible," I said. "I was thinking of going."

She smiled, looping her arm through mine for a brief moment. "Well then, if you're going... girls' night?"

"Girls' night," I echoed, the words settling warm and easy between us.

We parted at the corner.

Snow fell in slow, weightless spirals—and for a moment, it almost looked like memory falling.

Chapter Nine

CHAPTER NINE

The lobby of the Valérie Duval show glowed like the inside of a champagne bottle—warm gold, soft fizz, and the hum of editors, stylists, and industry insiders who only ever appeared at events worth remembering. Cameras flashed in polite bursts, catching on sequins, satin, and the polished marble floors. Even the air smelled exquisite—bergamot, orchids, and the faint heat of runway lights warming up.

Biljana and I stepped inside together, our coats whisked away by attendants who moved with the seamless efficiency of people trained in couture environments. For a moment, neither of us spoke. The space was breathtaking—Duval's signature. A world built for beauty, craft, and spectacle.

"This is insane," Biljana murmured beside me, tugging off her gloves.

The winter-white silk of her blouse caught the chandelier light and glowed faintly, elegant but effortless—very her.

"This is Duval," I said, smiling. "She doesn't do small."

Ushers guided us toward the inner hall—a vaulted expanse transformed into a runway that felt more like an art installation. Above, crimson lighting built in soft gradients, like the inside of a heart-beat. The front row gleamed with lacquered invitations bearing the show's title in looping cursive:

Love Affair

A Winter Collection by Valérie Duval

The title suited her—romantic, bold, slightly dangerous. And tonight, that energy hung in the air like perfume.

We found our seats two rows back, close enough to see every stitch, far enough for the mystery to stay intact. Miko appeared just then, sliding into the seat beside us with an easy grin—handsome in the way men in this world always seemed aware of.

"You two clean up well," he said, leaning in for a kiss on each cheek.

"You're here too?" Biljana asked.

"Of course. Half my models are walking." He smirked. "Duval begged."

I rolled my eyes. "You rehearsing lines in the car?"

He laughed low. "You missed me."

I didn't answer. I didn't need to.

The lights dipped. A hush swept over the room—the unified inhale of hundreds of people who pretended not to care but absolutely did. The first notes of the soundtrack pulsed softly beneath the dark, like fabric unfurling. Then the runway ignited.

A model emerged from the shadows, draped head to toe in liquid red silk, the fabric catching the light like flame. Another followed—a structured coat in deep crimson, cinched with glossy patent leather. Then another—ruby sequins, scarlet satin, Bordeaux velvet.

Row after row of red.

It was mesmerizing. Bold. Cohesive.

But also... unsettling.

All that red—unbroken, unrelenting—felt like a pulse echoing somewhere far beneath my ribs. A memory I couldn't place tugged upward, blurring the edges of the runway.

And then she appeared.

A model glided forward in a long, red silk scarf, the fabric trailing behind her like a ribbon of fire.

My stomach dipped—

not from the beauty of it,

not from Duval's theatrics,

but because—

There it was again.

Another red scarf.

The third in a row.

A poster at the gala.

A memory I couldn't quite place.

Laura's offhand story at the café.

And now this.

"Wow," Biljana whispered beside me. "That's stunning."

I swallowed hard. "Yeah... stunning." But my voice didn't sound like mine.

Why did this keep happening?

Why did the sight of a simple scarf make something inside me tighten—quiet, uneasy, like a warning I couldn't interpret?

I tried to blink it away, to chalk it up to a coincidence, but the unease lingered—low, steady, impossible to name.

The music deepened, vibrating through the floorboards in a slow, hypnotic thrum as the models rotated through the final looks, each silhouette a variation of the same red theme: flowing, structured, architectural, barely there. The room watched with rapt attention, but the lights felt too bright now, too sharp, the colors too saturated.

I shifted in my seat. It felt like the edges of the world were glinting—not breaking, not yet, just… shimmering in a way that made me second-guess my own eyes.

Beside me, Miko leaned forward, elbows on his knees, fully absorbed in the runway.

"She's rewriting the whole season," he murmured. "This is going to explode in Europe."

Biljana nodded, entranced. "It's breathtaking. Honestly, she's a genius."

Maybe it was genius. Or maybe it was something else.

The next model appeared in a structured crimson gown, the fabric folding like origami around her frame—a walking sculpture. The audience gasped softly, charmed and impressed.

But I watched the way the spotlight flickered—not enough for the crowd to notice, but just enough for me to feel the smallest tremor beneath my ribs.

Then another flicker.

Barely a heartbeat.

Like a skipped frame in a film.

I blinked, refocused.

The runway looked normal again. Beautiful, even. Maybe it was just the lighting. Or fatigue. Or the ghost of too many red scarves haunting the corners of my vision.

Still, the sense remained—

a hum beneath my skin,

a whisper of recognition I couldn't quite place.

Miko brushed a hand along his jaw. "She'll end with something dramatic. She always does."

And she did.

The finale model swept forward in a gown so red it bordered on violent—a sculptural masterpiece trailing yards of fabric behind her, catching the air like smoke unfolding after a spark.

The room erupted in applause, rising like a physical wave.

Everyone stood.

I rose with the others, clapping, though my palms were damp and my breath came unevenly. The applause sounded distant, like it was coming from far away.

Biljana nudged me playfully. "Earth to Amanda. You okay?"

I forced a small laugh. "Yeah. Just overwhelmed. It was... a lot."

She smiled and linked her arm through mine as the crowd began to spill toward the lobby.

"Come on. Let's get a drink before we face the cold."

But as we walked, surrounded by chatter and camera flashes, I kept glancing back toward the runway—expecting to see the scarf again.

Expecting it to mean something.

Expecting it to explain itself.

But it was gone.

Only the lingering hum remained.

A quiet echo.

A small fracture.

A red thread tugging somewhere I couldn't see.

The crowd surged toward the grand foyer, voices rising in warm waves of praise and commentary—fashion editors dissecting silhouettes, stylists already predicting which gowns would dominate red-carpet season. The whole place pulsed with admiration.

I should've felt it, too. I should've been swept up in the excitement, in the privilege of witnessing a Duval show up close. But something inside me felt slightly slanted, as if the room had tilted by just a degree or two, throwing off my balance in ways no one else noticed.

I tried to shake it off.

It was just a scarf.

Just a color.

Just a coincidence.

But my chest stayed tight with that quiet, inexplicable pressure—unease curling low and patient beneath my ribs.

Biljana kept her arm through mine as we followed the crowd. "I can't believe how good that was," she said, practically glowing. "I feel like we just watched history."

"I know," I replied, though my voice came out thinner than I meant. "It was... unforgettable."

She studied me for a moment. "You sure you're okay?"

"Yeah," I lied lightly. "Just lightheaded. Too much champagne at lunch, maybe."

She nudged me. "Then we'll get you food."

We stepped into the reception hall—a sweeping, high-ceilinged space draped in soft blush lighting. Caterers in crisp black carried trays of champagne, truffle canapés, and blood-orange cocktails that matched the show's palette. A Duval signature: nothing ever clashed.

Miko rejoined us, brushing past an editor to snag two glasses of champagne. He handed one to me.

"Drink. You look like you need it."

I gave another forced laugh. "Is it that obvious?"

"A little." He took a sip from his own glass. "Duval's productions overwhelm everyone. Even me. And I'm professionally un-overwhelmable."

I rolled my eyes, grateful for the banter. "Is that a word?"

He winked. "It is when I say it."

The lightness grounded me—just enough for my breath to steady.

But then a waiter passed, carrying a tray of garnet-colored cocktails, and the deep red of the drink caught the light in a way that made my pulse skip.

Another red.

Everywhere, red.

I blinked and looked away.

"Hey," Miko said quietly, his voice warm. "You're really not yourself tonight."

"I'm fine," I said—too quickly.

Biljana reappeared with a trio of tiny plates. "Food," she announced, offering one to me. "Eat. Please. You look pale."

The concern in her face made something in me soften, settle.

"Thanks," I said, taking a small bite of the tartlet and letting the richness distract me. "I'm fine. Really. The finale just... hit me weird, I guess."

"Hit you weird how?" she asked.

I shook my head. "I don't know. Maybe it was the lighting. Or the way everything was so... red. It was overwhelming."

"That's the point," Miko said with a shrug. "Duval loves saturation. The critics call it sensory immersion. I call it chaos with a good tailor."

Biljana laughed. "Accurate."

I smiled—genuinely this time—but the unease still trickled beneath the surface.

Because as they spoke, my eyes drifted toward the empty runway, still visible through the open doors. The red scarf lay draped over a mannequin in the corner now, artfully placed for photo ops, the ends cascading like a ribbon of blood on ice-white marble.

And something in me whispered again—too soft to name, too loud to ignore.

"Amanda?" Biljana's voice pulled me back.

"Mm?"

"Come on," she said, nodding toward the far corner. "There's a little photo installation. Duval's team is doing Polaroids of guests. It'll be cute."

"I don't really—"

"Just one," she said, tugging lightly at my hand. "For fun."

Fun. Right.

I followed them—Miko sauntering ahead, Biljana's excitement infectious. But as we neared the installation, I caught a reflection of myself in a mirrored column: elegant, composed... yet my eyes looked a shade too wide, like they were trying to gather more light than the room could give.

Something pulled at me again— quiet, insistent. The feeling that the world was becoming thinner at the edges. Not broken. Not yet. Just stretched, like fabric pulled taut before a seam gives way.

I took a slow breath, letting it out through parted lips as I drifted toward the edge of the room.

The crowd moved like a single organism—shimmering, laughing, brushing past in waves of perfume and velvet. I tried to let the energy wash over me, to shake loose the strange tightness in my chest.

It was just a scarf. Just a memory. Just... nothing. Or that's what I told myself.

I reached for a glass from a passing tray—something sparkling, cold enough to fog the stem—and stepped toward a quieter corner near a cluster of orchids arranged in a blown-glass vase. Their petals glowed under the soft lighting, pale and delicate against the relentless red surrounding us.

"Beautiful, aren't they?" a voice said beside me.

I turned to find an older woman—silver hair swept into an elegant knot, crimson lipstick impeccable. She looked familiar in the way fashion veterans often do: someone who had attended every show worth remembering, someone who had lived a dozen lives before the rest of us ever caught up.

"Yes," I said, offering a polite smile. "They're stunning."

She nodded once, studying me with an attention that felt both gentle and sharp.

"You felt that shift tonight, didn't you?" she asked, her tone conversational, as if commenting on the weather.

I blinked. "Shift?"

"The mood," she said with a faint shrug, lifting her champagne. "Some collections speak; others whisper. But this one..." Her eyes traveled back to the runway, now empty except for crumbs of glittering fabric left behind. "This one stirred something. You could feel it."

I didn't know what to say, so I only nodded. Her gaze softened, as though she'd expected the silence.

"Red is a memory color," she added, her voice quieter now. "Designers forget that sometimes. Couture can dazzle, but certain shades carry echoes. They remind us of things we never meant to remember."

Something in my stomach tightened.

Before I could respond, Miko's voice cut through the noise behind me.

"There you are," he said, slipping an arm lightly around my shoulder with a warmth that grounded me. "I thought we lost you to the orchid garden."

I turned back—but the woman was already gliding away, her champagne glass catching the light like a small comet.

"Who was that?" Miko asked, following my gaze.

"I... don't know," I said honestly. "Someone who really loves orchids."

He laughed, smooth and easy. "This entire room loves orchids. And themselves."

I tried to laugh too, but something about her words clung to me. Not the orchids. Not the red.

The memory part.

The echo part.

Miko brushed a speck of glitter from my sleeve. "Come on. Biljana's talking to the Duval team and making friends with the head stylist. We should rescue them before she negotiates herself into the next show."

I let him guide me back through the crowd, my heels clicking softly against the polished floor. And for the rest of the night—through the laughter, the mingling, the easy glamour of it all—I kept catching glimpses of red.

A coat.

A cocktail dress.

A ribbon pinned into someone's hair.

All harmless.

All ordinary.

And yet each one landed with a small, inexplicable weight inside me.

I told myself it was just the aesthetic of the night—Duval's vision lingering like perfume in the air.

We drifted back toward Biljana as the crowd thinned into small constellations of people with champagne flutes and curated smiles.

The three of us regrouped near the lobby doors, the night settling around us in soft, glittering folds.

"Ready to head out?" Miko asked, looping his scarf around his neck.

Biljana nodded. "Our car should be waiting."

I slipped into my coat, forcing my breath to steady. But as we stepped into the cold, the city lights scattering in the melting snow, I couldn't shake the tiny, persistent unease curled beneath my skin.

Red was everywhere suddenly. And I no longer believed it was a coincidence.

Outside, the winter air met us—sharp and clean. Limos pulled up in tidy choreography, headlights glowing against the falling snow. Biljana squeezed my arm, warmth threading through the cold.

"Tonight was fun," she said. "We needed this."

"Yeah," I answered. "We did."

As we moved toward the waiting car, the city stirred around us—elegant, humming, utterly ordinary. And yet, a quiet tremor threaded through me, the faintest ripple at the edge of everything familiar.

Not fear. Not certainty. Just that same small whisper. Something's coming.

By the time the door shut behind us and the car eased into traffic, I'd smoothed my expression back into something calm and composed. A woman on her way home from a glamorous night out.

But the truth followed like a soft echo: something had shifted tonight.

I could feel it—subtle, unmistakable—as though the world had tilted a single degree, just enough for everything to catch the light differently. Just enough for memory to feel... closer.

Chapter Ten

CHAPTER TEN

The week between Christmas and New Year's always felt like living inside a dream—whimsical and bright, yet threaded with reflection. A week suspended between what was and what might be, when everyone seemed to look inward, measuring the distance between who they were and who they hoped to become.

This year, though, I already knew.

This chapter would be different; it was time to step into the new and leave the what-ifs behind.

Earlier that evening, over dinner with Biljana and Miko, they told me they were finally ready to step into the spotlight together—as a couple. And for the first time, I felt no ache in hearing it, only a quiet, genuine happiness. It was as if all three of us were turning the page at once—separately, but also together.

Later, as I walked home through the city's winter glow, a lightness stirred in me that I hadn't known in years. Hope returned—soft, unhurried—the kind that doesn't demand, only waits. I didn't know when or how, but I knew I was ready: ready to let someone new in, ready to believe that love could arrive quietly this time, without the past following close behind.

Back home, I slipped off my heels and stood by the window, the city lights glittering below like distant stars scattered across glass. The night hummed with a kind of muffled life—horns calling faintly from far-off avenues, music drifting from a passing car, the low murmur of a city that never really sleeps. Somewhere below, a car horn sounded, voices rose from the street, and I realized how alive everything felt again.

I leaned closer to the window, my breath fogging the glass before fading. The pane was cold beneath my fingertips—grounding and distant all at once. I traced a small circle in the condensation and watched it vanish, as if even my touch couldn't hold shape for long. Maybe that was how it was meant to be—some things appearing only long enough to remind you they were there.

The faint glow of my apartment wrapped around me—soft lamps, half-melted candles from Christmas Eve, the scent of pine still clinging to the air. My coat was draped over the arm of the chair, a silk ribbon from a gift half-tucked beneath it. The room felt lived-in, paused, mid-story.

I poured the last of the wine from the bottle I'd opened earlier in the week, the sound soft and familiar. Outside, snow had started falling again—barely there at first, small flecks catching the streetlight as they drifted down like confetti, too tired to celebrate. I smiled at the thought.

Tomorrow would bring the final preparations for the gala—the fittings, the phone calls, the swirl of plans pulling me back into the current of who I was expected to be. But tonight, in this quiet moment suspended between holidays, I let myself simply exist—no performance, no pretense, no need to be anything at all.

The world outside sparkled in motion, but I stood still, the chill of the window seeping into my skin, the calm of it settling somewhere deeper. Tonight—tonight was still mine.

Chapter Eleven

CHAPTER ELEVEN

The morning of the party was hectic in all the best ways—the kind of chaos that felt alive. Phones buzzed, deliveries arrived, and voices overlapped in bursts of excitement. We had vendors and coordinators handling every detail now, but I still wanted to be there.

Biljana had long since given up the early mornings, trusting the planners to bring the vision to life. But I couldn't stay away. Maybe it was a habit. Maybe it was control. Or maybe it was the quiet satisfaction of watching an idea—something that once existed only in sketches and color swatches—take shape right before my eyes.

The ballroom transformed piece by piece: candlelight glinting off crystal vases, white calla lilies unfurling in tall glass towers. It never failed to take my breath away, that first glimpse when everything aligned—the scent of fresh blooms, the soft rustle of fabric, the faint echo of a playlist testing through the speakers. For a moment, the world outside didn't exist.

After making one last round with the staff and giving an approving nod to the lighting techs, I glanced at my phone—already past noon. I was running late. Typical. With one last look at the ballroom,

I hurried out and slipped into the waiting car. My hair and makeup artist would already be setting up by the time I got home.

It wasn't the first time I'd raced the clock to get ready—years of modeling had trained me to move fast, to make chaos look effortless. And today would be no different.

The apartment was alive with motion—brushes clicking against glass palettes, the low hum of blow-dryers, soft laughter from the makeup team as they worked their quiet magic. Afternoon light streamed through the floor-to-ceiling windows, spilling over the marble floors and glinting off the half-filled flutes of champagne scattered across the console table.

This part of the day had always felt familiar, almost ritualistic—the transformation from the inside out. Years of modeling had trained me to move through it without thinking, to let others craft the image the world expected. But today, something about the rhythm felt off. The chatter around me blurred into white noise, and for a moment, I missed the sound of Biljana's voice—the quick, sharp wit that usually filled the space when we got ready together.

The phone buzzed on the coffee table. Biljana.

I smiled, answering before the second ring. "Tell me you're not still reviewing briefs on New Year's Eve."

A laugh, warm and knowing. "Caught me. Just one last file. Then I promise I'll put the lawyer away and let the party girl out."

"Good," I teased. "You've got fireworks to host and champagne to sip. The city can survive without your cross-examinations for one night."

"I'll hold you to that," she said lightly. "Miko's already at the Ritz, overseeing the soundcheck. You know how he is—'everything must be perfect.'"

I laughed. "Of course he is. Remind him the flowers are my jurisdiction—if he starts rearranging them, I'll revoke his creative privileges."

She laughed again, that familiar melodic sound that always made things feel lighter. "Duly noted."

When the call ended, I sat back as one of the stylists smoothed a final curl into place. The city stretched out before me—glass, steel, light. From up here, everything looked orderly, contained. But somewhere beneath that perfection, something restless stirred.

I reached for my champagne flute, took a slow sip, and said quietly to no one in particular—half a joke, half a promise: "Tonight will be perfect. Memorable."

The words lingered in the air, light as bubbles, before sinking under their own weight. Somewhere deep down, I already knew—perfection never lasts.

The city shimmered outside the car window as we pulled up to the Ritz. The entrance blazed beneath tiers of light, the kind that made every arriving guest look briefly cinematic. Valets darted between sleek black cars; laughter rose above the low hum of traffic, the air sharp with winter and anticipation.

Inside, the ballroom unfolded in layers of black and gold—panels of dark velvet broken by mirrored columns, candles burning low inside crystal holders, and towering arrangements of white lilies glowing against the darker backdrop. Every surface seemed to breathe light—not soft or romantic, but electric, alive.

For a moment, I just stood there, letting it all wash over me. This—the shimmer, the music, the pulse—was the world I understood. The world I'd built.

"Finally!" Biljana's voice rose above the crowd. She crossed the room in a sweep of rose-gold sequins that caught every flicker of light, her hair swept into a glossy knot, a champagne flute balanced effortlessly in her hand. Miko followed close behind, cufflinks glinting as he adjusted them, the picture of composed ease.

"You look stunning," I said, and meant it.

She smiled, tilting her head. "You too. Always the model."

Miko grinned. "See? I told you she'd outshine us both."

"Only because I had a head start," I teased, laughing. Around us, the room buzzed—clinking glasses, quick bursts of laughter, the tuning of instruments near the stage.

"Laura's here somewhere," Biljana said, scanning the crowd. "She texted that she was running fashionably late—some meeting ran over. Typical."

"Wouldn't be her if she didn't make an entrance," I said.

As if on cue, Laura appeared near the entrance, shrugging off her coat, a flash of deep red silk around her neck—a scarf that caught the light like fire.

Our eyes met, and she waved, weaving her way toward us.

Something in my chest tightened, though I couldn't have said why. That scarf again. Always the red.

Then, beneath the bass of the music, a faint tremor moved through the floor—so subtle I thought I'd imagined it. The chandeliers above swayed, their crystals whispering against each other before settling.

No one else seemed to notice.

Biljana turned toward the stage, raising her glass, her laughter blending seamlessly back into the crowd's.

I smiled too, though something inside me had shifted—a quiet, unnamable unease, the sense that the night was holding its breath.

PART II

The Ache Beneath

Chapter Twelve

CHAPTER TWELVE

Somewhere in the distance, thunder began to roar, and the ballroom windows shivered in their frames. Yet no one seemed to notice again. I felt caught in a moment that belonged only to me, while the world around me carried on, untouched.

I glanced at Biljana, expecting her to react, but she was leaning into Miko, laughing at something he said, perfectly at ease. Not even a flicker of concern.

The band played on, the rhythm moving through me like a pulse—until, just for a breath, it slipped. The space between notes stretched thin, and the faces on stage seemed to halt, dissolving at the edges as if the night itself were starting to forget its shape.

Another low rumble rolled through the floor, deeper this time. The chandeliers flickered above us, their light trembling across glass and faces below. It wasn't beautiful anymore—it was unsteady, as if something beneath the surface had shifted.

The music faltered again, slipping out of sync with itself, the notes dragging like they'd forgotten where to go. My chest tightened. The scent of perfume and champagne began to fade, replaced by something colder—like the charged, metallic air before a storm. The temperature dropped; the atmosphere grew heavier.

"Biljana?" I said, barely a whisper.

She turned toward me, her laughter fading mid-breath. For a moment, her smile lingered, but her eyes had already changed—wide, uncertain, searching for something that hadn't been there a second ago. The light trembled again, washing her face in alternating gold and shadow.

"Did you feel that?" she asked.

I forced a small smile and shook my head. "It's probably nothing," I said, though the words felt brittle the moment they left my mouth.

The floor shivered beneath us—a subtle vibration at first, like the hum of something enormous moving just beyond reach. Glasses trembled on tables. A few people glanced around, their hesitant smiles beginning to falter. Another tremor passed, stronger this time—the kind you feel before you hear it.

Biljana reached for my hand, her fingers cold against mine. "Maybe we should—"

The lights flickered once more, then steadied, casting the room in a dim, uncertain glow. For a heartbeat, no one moved.

The rumble deepened, moving through the glassware and beneath the floor—a low vibration that filled the room like a held breath. The chandeliers above swayed, scattering light that danced once, then fractured. I looked up just as one crystal teardrop loosened and fell, catching the light on its way down before vanishing into shadow.

Then, without warning, the world began to change.

The marble floor seemed to melt away, revealing warm parquet beneath—narrow oak pieces laid in a herringbone pattern, soft with age and memory.

The tall windows shuddered, their grand arches narrowing into familiar French frames, the glass paling with frost. Velvet curtains shimmered, then thinned into sheer linen, drifting in a draft I could suddenly feel against my arms. The tables dimmed too—centerpieces of crystal and gold softening into vases of calla lilies, their white petals catching the last of the flickering light.

Above, the chandelier flickered once, then again, its glow fading to a soft, unsteady light. The music stumbled, slowing to a crawl before vanishing altogether. For a moment, there was only silence—and the faint, distant hum of something else.

A vibration moved through the floorboards, steady and real. When I looked up, the chandeliers were gone. In their place hung a single crystal fixture, its light trembling gently across the walls. The ballroom's glittering expanse had folded inward—shrinking, softening—until all that remained was a modest room with parquet floors, French windows, and sheer linen curtains stirring faintly in the stillness.

By the window, a vase of calla lilies stood untouched. Their white petals glowed in the half-light, unchanged by the world around them.

Somewhere outside, a sound rumbled—a low, distant roar that trembled through the glass. Not thunder this time. Something closer. Something real.

Chapter Thirteen

CHAPTER THIRTEEN

"I don't want to imagine and pretend anymore!" Ela's voice cracked as she tugged the red scarf from her shoulders and let it fall to the floor. The sound it made—soft, final—tightened my stomach.

"I'm too scared, Lana. It's not working anymore. Did you hear the fighter jets in the distance? The boom shook the windows again. I don't think we're safe tonight."

I tried to steady her with my eyes, even as mine kept drifting toward the glass, wondering if the tape would hold. We'd learned in school how to crisscross tape across windows, how to stack sandbags around doors and walls to absorb shockwaves and blast shards. At school, it was just a lesson. At home, it was something you did with your family to feel a little safer.

Ela and I had taped these French windows ourselves, our small hands smoothing down strips that looked flimsy against the sky-breaking sound. Somehow, it had felt like we were protecting our sanctuary—the room where we imagined everything and escaped reality in hopeful dreams.

"We'll be okay," I said. "The news said the holiday ceasefire across Croatia will hold until tomorrow—at least that's what they promised. Tonight, we're safe."

Her big blue eyes searched mine, desperate for proof I wasn't just saying words to make her feel better. Waiting for the kind of certainty no one really had here.

Deep down, I already knew what I couldn't say out loud: ceasefires were fragile things. They broke like glass. After nearly a year of war, I didn't need to be an adult to understand that. I could feel it—even in the silence of our small room—the way the air carried a weight, as if holding its breath, waiting for the inevitable.

Still, I clung to the story. Tonight had to be different. Both our parents were home, sitting together in the living room. That hadn't happened in months. They were watching the evening news, waiting for the "Countdown to 1992" program to begin. Just like a normal family. For one night, I wanted to believe in normal.

I picked up the scarf and handed it back to Ela. "It looks beautiful on you. Remember, you're strong. Don't let fear take this from us—not tonight."

But it was already too late.

The lights flickered once, then the apartment plunged into darkness—another blackout. We were used to them by now. Darkness meant the city had disappeared, hidden from the fighter planes above. Yet the silence that followed never felt safe; it only warned that the worst was on its way.

Chapter Fourteen

CHAPTER FOURTEEN

The air raid sirens cut through the darkness—high-pitched and piercing—splitting the night like a knife. By now, I should've been used to it. We'd heard them before. We'd run before. But something in me tightened anyway. Maybe it was because it was New Year's Eve. Maybe because both Mom and Dad were here tonight, together, like things used to be. For once, I'd let myself believe we were safe.

Ela smacked her hands over her ears, eyes wide and glossy. The sirens howled too loudly to comfort her with words. I could only look at her and pretend I wasn't just as scared.

I heard the pounding of footsteps before the door burst open. Flashlight beams cut across the dark. Their faces told me everything—the tightness of fear in their expressions, the urgency in their eyes. Dad clutched his old leather briefcase, the one stuffed with documents, papers, proof of our lives—everything we'd need if the building was hit and we had to run for good. That briefcase never left his side when the sirens started.

"Ela, Lana—now!" Dad shouted, his voice splintering against the shriek of sirens.

And even though we'd run this drill before, even though I knew exactly what to do, something inside me whispered this night was different. I couldn't shake it. Something different was coming.

As we joined our neighbors in the stairwell, the first illumination flares went up with a roar—like a rocket tearing the sky open. For a second, I thought it was a bomb. But then the light burst overhead, flooding everything in a ghostly white glow. False daylight rushed through the sky like wildfire, devouring the dark and leaving nowhere to hide. The hiss as it drifted down on its parachute was almost worse than the silence before.

That was when the panic began. Neighbors surged down the stairwell—voices breaking, feet pounding. Someone screamed, and the press of bodies shoved us forward. I clutched Ela's hand so tightly her fingers must've hurt, but if I let go, we'd lose each other in the crowd. The stairwell echoed with fear, with the sound of people stumbling over one another in their rush to get below ground before the next flare—or the bombs that always seemed to follow.

"Dad!" Ela screamed as I tried to hold her against me.

Luckily, Mom was within reach, pulling Ela's small hand away from the flimsy railing. Dad was right behind me, urging me to keep going. Now more than ever, all any of us could think about was escaping the building and getting to shelter.

When we reached the ground floor, panic splintered in every direction—people lunged for doors and windows, desperate to escape faster than their bodies could move.

Above us, a flare drifted down on its parachute, spilling smoke into the building until the air itself seemed to choke. Screams rose—sharper, louder—as no one knew whether it was only smoke or something far worse creeping in with it. Then, finally, the front doors gave way, and the crowd poured out, vanishing into the streets.

Chapter Fifteen

CHAPTER FIFTEEN

My mom scooped Ela into her arms, and my dad gripped my hand.

"Hold on tight—don't let go, and don't stop running," he told me, his voice urgent.

The nearest shelter was only two city blocks away, tucked beneath the great cultural arts center. By day, its glass walls shimmered with sunlight, displaying paintings and sculptures that gave us hope. We used to go there on field trips, proof that something human still remained in the world. Now, that same building was our only chance at survival.

We sprinted into the street. Fighter jets tore across the sky, their roar rattling in my chest. More flares exploded overhead, flooding the city with false daylight so the planes could see their targets more clearly. Behind us, tank treads chewed the ground, their thunder shaking through my jaw.

The first bombs struck nearby—light split the sky, buildings shuddered. Our sector was next. Dad's grip crushed my hand as he dragged me forward, desperate to outrun the fire closing in. We were still a block and a half from the shelter. Too far.

Croatian military police shouted, waving us toward safety, but the street was chaos—people scattering, stumbling, terror carved into their faces. Mom clutched Ela against her chest, rushing just ahead of us. Over her shoulder, I saw Ela's face, pale and wide-eyed with fear.

Then came the gunfire. Bullets cracked through the air, snapping past in front and behind. I didn't know where they were coming from—only that they were chasing us too. Ela screamed and buried her face in Mom's shoulder, as if hiding there could erase the nightmare pressing in.

But I couldn't close my eyes. I was old enough to run, and old enough to know I had no choice.

Run and live. Stop and die. That was all I could think.

My lungs burned. My legs dragged heavier with every step. Dad pulled harder, urging me on.

"Lana! Faster—hold on tighter!"

But I was starting to fall behind. My vision blurred, ears rang. My hand slipped from his.

And then I lost it.

I stumbled, hitting the ground just as another blast ripped the street apart. The shockwave slammed me flat against the earth. For one endless moment, I couldn't tell if I was alive or already gone—caught somewhere in between, where time stopped, the world blurred, and every sound was muffled into silence.

It lasted only seconds, but inside that hollow eternity, I thought I was already lost.

Chapter Sixteen

CHAPTER SIXTEEN

"Lana! Lana!" Dad's voice cut through the fog, sharp enough to drag me back to reality.

Ahead, I caught sight of Ela's face over Mom's shoulder, and the adrenaline surged again, yanking me to my feet. We weren't out of danger. Not yet.

Dad glanced at me—just for a second—as if he wanted to stop, to check if I was hurt. But we both knew there was no time. Not until we reached the shelter.

We kept running as bombs fell, their thunder rolling through the air, until the art center finally loomed ahead. The sight of it sent a tremor of relief through me. I heard Mom's voice, breathless but steady, whisper, "Thank God we are here."

Inside, a wave of relief swept through my tense body. For the first time all night, I could be still.

But then Mom's eyes landed on me. "Lana," she whispered, her voice trembling. Ela peeked over her shoulder and gasped, "You're bleeding!" Only then did I feel the sting in my hand—raw and scraped from the fall.

Dad crouched without a word, pulling the battered first aid kit from the wall. His hands moved quickly, cleaning and bandaging as the din of footsteps and whispers echoed around us. When he finished, Mom pulled both Ela and me into her arms, holding us so tightly I could feel her fear shaking through her chest. Tears streaked her cheeks as she whispered, "Too close... too close."

The shelter grew more crowded by the second. And though I knew what was coming, I never wanted to think about it. Even as a child, I understood the rhythm of war. Relief never lasted. Every breath of safety was only borrowed, and anguish always waited to take it back.

And then it came.

With a final groan of metal, the shelter guard sealed the heavy door and told us it would not open—not for any reason—until the all-clear siren sounded.

The room fell silent, though the bombs still shuddered through the distance, their force muffled by concrete walls. Moments later, the banging began—fists pounding against the metal, voices rising in desperate pleas to be let in.

No one moved. No one spoke. Adults kept their eyes on the floor, their silence thick with guilt and shame. We, children, felt it too—the weight pressing down on our chests, the helplessness carved into the air.

They would always call us children. But in that moment, I knew I wasn't one anymore. War had taken that from me.

The truth was, we had already let in more people than the shelter could safely hold. Any more, and we risked running out of oxygen—or worse, a stampede.

Still, the fists kept pounding, the voices growing hoarse, their desperation echoing through the concrete walls. Each blow against the metal door rattled inside my chest, a brutal reminder that safety for us meant abandonment for them.

Ela's wide eyes turned to me, searching my face for permission to move, to help, to do something. But I had nothing to give her—no comfort, no answer. Only silence, just like the adults.

It was inevitable. And it was gut-wrenching.

Chapter Seventeen

CHAPTER SEVENTEEN

Finally, the banging stopped. The sudden quiet pressed against my ears until Ela whispered, "Do you think they found another shelter?"

There were other shelters in the area—I knew that much. And I wanted to believe the silence meant safety. "Yes," I told her. "They must have."

Ela leaned into me, comforted by the thought. Dad's eyes found mine in the dim room. He gave the smallest nod, as if to say I'd done the right thing—that we would believe in that hope together, even if we could never be sure.

The next hours blurred into a strange rhythm, whispers and prayers stitched between the distant thud of shells. Every so often, the ceiling trembled, flecks of white paint drifting down like brittle snow. Shadows of fear moved across the faces around us, but inside our small circle, in the corner, we clung to something else.

I leaned close to Ela and whispered, "What do you think Amanda and Biljana are doing right now?"

Her eyes lit with the fragile spark I needed to see. So we began again—piecing together their world, dress by dress, dream by dream, building a life that was everything ours was not.

In an instant, the shelter walls dissolved. I was Amanda, standing beneath the glow of chandeliers, the gala alive with laughter and crystal light. The DJ spun the music, inviting everyone to the dance floor. Biljana swept me into the rhythm, and for a moment, I forgot the strange shadows that had flickered just before. I let myself go, my laughter rising, carried by the pulse of the music.

Across the floor, Miko caught sight of us. He grinned and slipped through the crowd until he reached the dance floor, joining our circle. The three of us spun beneath the glittering light, laughter spilling as we twirled, the air alive with a shimmer of anticipation for the final countdown to the new year.

Then the chandeliers shook. Glass rained down like falling stars. A deafening blast ripped through the air—close. Too close.

The shelter shuddered. Cries broke out, and the fantasy shattered in an instant. We were back underground, cold concrete and fear pressing in on every side.

That was how shelter life was—you never knew what was coming next, only that you were as safe as you could be. We clung to each other in silence until, at last, the all-clear siren echoed through the air around 11 p.m.

Each time it sounded, emotions surged high again—a mixture of relief and the gnawing anxiety of not knowing what waited outside.

The sound of feet shuffling in silence filled the space as the shelter guard unlocked the heavy steel door. When it swung open, night rushed in—thick with the aftermath of bombing and shelling. Smoke hung low in the cold air, laced with a fine dusting of fresh snow. It was beautiful and dreadful all at once.

Debris and glass littered the streets. Smoke curled up from not-too-distant buildings and bled into the dark sky.

As we began the walk home, I heard the voices around us—whimpers, whispered prayers, even quiet curses muttered into the night. Sadness, anger, and hope moved together in one heavy current. Every step pulled us closer to our apartment, and all we could think about was whether it still stood. I heard Mom praying under her breath, her words tumbling into the cold as if they might keep our home intact.

Our block finally came into view. Smoke poured from the building next door. A sigh of relief escaped me—our building was safe. The one beside it was not.

The ground floor had been a small community pharmacy, the top floor a shop. I heard Dad murmur to Mom, his voice tight, about the worry of losing medicine and supplies so close by. The shelves had already been bare most days, but now there would be nothing to find at all. There were others in the city, yes—but this had been ours, the one we all depended on.

As we entered our building, shattered glass crunched beneath our feet. Lights dangled above, swinging like fragile pendulums. Every window was blown out, the night air rushing through the atrium in icy gusts. The walls seemed to weep, streaked with shell holes and powdered fragments drifting loose.

Dad lifted Ela into his arms and turned to me.

"Lana—watch where you step."

The stairwell railing bowed, cracked, and scarred from the weight of bodies pressed against it and the force of shelling that had cut through.

When we stepped inside, cold air rushed through the broken windows, carrying the smell of dust and smoke into every corner. For a moment, none of us spoke—we only looked.

Ela and I stood frozen in the middle of the entryway, our eyes darting across the open living room we'd once called our playroom. The walls seemed to weep, streaked with hairline cracks and powdered plaster drifting down in slow breaths. Shards of glass littered the floor, catching what little light remained, sharp and glittering like scattered stars.

Mom moved first, her hands trembling as she began to steady the fallen objects in the kitchen—cups tipped, a bowl cracked clean in two, flour spilling like snow across the counter. Dad bent low without a word, sweeping glass and debris into neat piles, his motions brisk and controlled. It was what we all did after the bombs: find order in the wreckage.

The damage wasn't from a direct hit—we'd been spared that—but from the tremors that rattled through whenever bombs struck nearby. By now, it felt almost ordinary, the way plaster cracked and ceilings shed dust, as if the building itself bore the shudders of war.

Amid the splinters, the calla lilies lay tipped from their vase, scattered in fragile arcs. Their white petals remained unmarked, untouched by the chaos outside. In their quiet perfection, I saw proof that even in the darkest moments, beauty—and hope—could survive.

Beside them, half-buried in dust, lay the red scarf. Its color still bled through the gray, a thread of brightness against the ruin. It looked wounded yet defiant, refusing to vanish beneath the rubble.

Ela darted toward it, snatching it up with small, determined hands. She shook off the gray powder clinging to its fabric, then pressed it against her cheek with a brave little smile.

"Biljana needs this for her next gala," she said, as if reminding us all that the story wasn't lost—not yet.

I gave her a smile back, letting the fantasy of hope stand.

Chapter Eighteen

CHAPTER EIGHTEEN

The next few days blurred together in smoke and dust. Crews moved through the city—workers, soldiers, neighbors with shovels—pushing debris into heaps and clearing just enough of the streets for cars to pass and children to walk to school again. It wasn't restoration, not really. In a war zone, you didn't rebuild—you made things barely passable, and that was enough to call it progress.

Returning to school after the holidays was supposed to help us find normal again—to keep us moving forward, even when some of us felt there was nothing left to give. A few classmates had lost fathers, brothers, friends. Others were still waiting for news of relatives gone missing. But still, we went to school.

Rituals and small duties helped. That week, it was my turn to clean the chalkboard, so I arrived early to wipe it down, to make sure it was fresh for the morning's lessons. The duty passed from one of us to the next, a small cycle of order we could count on. I didn't know why, but I liked the task. Something about washing the slate clean, about erasing what had been scribbled there, gave me the sense that I could control at least one small thing. For a moment, it felt like proof that life could begin again—unmarked.

As I scrubbed, the sound of footsteps filled the hall. The others were arriving—slipping off their street shoes, trading them for school slippers, lining the shelves with muddy boots that carried the outside world.

A smile spread across my face as Ivana's voice reached me. In that moment, it was proof that something normal had returned. My best friend was alive and well—and that was all I needed to keep going.

"Ivana! You're okay!" I ran to her, excitement breaking through my chest.

"Lana! I tried to call you, but all the lines were down after the bombing."

"I know. It's okay," I said.

Our other friends began to gather, their faces wide-eyed with relief as they spotted one another, happiness spilling into the hallway like light through a cracked door. Even in that perfect moment of thankfulness and hope, I couldn't help but wonder: how long before another attack tore it all away?

Chapter Nineteen

CHAPTER NINETEEN

Something about that morning's lesson felt brighter, happier—more inviting than usual. Smiles came easier, and for a moment, eagerness to do something normal filled the room. It was as if we were giving ourselves permission, just this once, to be kids again. We leaned forward, attentive and ready—to learn, to discuss, to grow.

And yet, even in that classroom, the reminders of war were everywhere. The windows stood fractured, panes missing like pieces of stolen hope. Sandbags pressed hard against the walls, as if trying to hold back the war itself.

After a brief welcome-back speech, we opened our math books and prepared for the lesson. In true fashion, the teacher began with an oral exam at the chalkboard. Naturally, she called on me. My stomach tightened the way it always did in these moments, but today, I welcomed it. I rose and walked to the front of the class with a strange kind of eagerness.

She wrote the problem neatly on the board and handed me the chalk. I studied it, then worked out the answer: 3. Stepping back, I realized my mistake almost instantly. Heart quickening, I erased the 3 and replaced it with a firm 4. I stood waiting, chalk dust still clinging to my fingers, as the teacher reviewed my work.

She nodded, then wrote down my grade. "B," she said, her tone even. "Your first answer was incorrect, even though you corrected it quickly."

It was harsh, yes—but also completely normal in Croatian schools. And in a strange way, that normalcy comforted me. For the first time in what felt like forever, I thought, *This feels good*. School was back in session, and I hadn't realized how much I needed it.

The teacher continued the oral exam, calling on a few more students in turn. None of us groaned or shifted in our seats the way we might have before. That day, no one seemed to mind. There was comfort in routine, even when it was strict.

When the last answer had been given, we moved into the lesson, hours folding quietly into one another. Numbers, words, and small questions filled the space—the familiar rhythm of school life washing over us like something we'd almost forgotten how to hold. For a little while, it felt almost ordinary.

But before the recess bell rang, the teacher's tone shifted. She told us that after lunch, we would have art. At first, a ripple of excitement moved through the room—art meant colors, brushes, freedom. Then came the twist: we would be drawing what war meant to us, what it felt like inside.

The words caught me off guard, stunned me into silence. Around me, whispers rose like dry leaves, scattering across the desks. I could tell I wasn't the only one who felt uneasy. Why now? Why drag us back down when we had just begun to forget—even for a moment—the world outside these walls?

Deep down, I knew the truth: it wasn't meant to wound us, but to give us space to let it out, to paint the unspoken. Still, it felt like betrayal—as if the fragile peace we had managed to stitch together in this classroom was about to be torn apart, thread by thread.

Chapter Twenty

CHAPTER TWENTY

The bell rang, and we pushed back from our desks. Lunch passed in a blur—chatter, scraps of laughter, the kind of noise that filled the cracks where fear usually lived. No one mentioned the art assignment. We didn't want to.

When recess began, Ivana and I slipped outside and claimed the bench by the basketball court. We leaned close, lost in girl talk—whispers about whose eyes lingered too long, whose smile held a promise, whose glance stirred something we didn't quite understand. For a few minutes, we were just two friends pretending life was simple.

Soon, a few more friends drifted over. We huddled together in the cold, trading laughter until the chill crept through our coats and left us shivering. To stay warm, we started walking, our feet carrying us toward the familiar trail behind the court.

It was the obvious choice—the shortcut through the woods that led to the wide stretch of the soccer field. A path we all knew by heart, the kind we never questioned. So we went, boots crunching on frozen ground, voices rising in playful bursts, carrying secrets and laughter into the hush of the trees.

As we moved deeper into the woods, the air grew heavier and cooler, like the weight of the world was suspended in that narrow stretch, pressing down on us. It was only a short patch of trees before the trail opened again into the field, but every time we walked it, our voices seemed to fade on their own. Sound didn't carry here. The path narrowed, branches leaning in, and we fell into a thinner line, almost single file.

I was out in front, setting the pace without meaning to, when something broke the pattern of earth and snow—a faint flicker of metal, sharp against the white, where the ground looked torn and pressed back, as if the earth itself were hiding a secret. For a moment, I told myself it was nothing, just a forgotten scrap. But each step closer pulled a knot tighter in my stomach, unease coiling like a warning I couldn't name.

"There's something here," I said, slowing down.

"What do you mean?" Ivana's voice wavered behind me.

"I don't know... it's odd, like a piece of metal or—" My words stopped as my stomach clenched. Just beneath the disturbed earth, a thin wire ran out, barely visible, almost swallowed by frost and dirt.

I froze, then stumbled back. "Stay back!" My voice cracked but rose loud enough to stop them. "We need to turn around. Now!"

Confusion broke out—shouts, questions—but fear moved faster. I was already running, and they followed, feet pounding the frozen earth.

"Don't go near it!" I shouted again, heart hammering. A couple of boys who had stepped closer caught sight of the wire. Their faces went pale. They didn't hesitate—they turned and sprinted with us toward the school.

Chapter Twenty-One

CHAPTER TWENTY-ONE

As we ran back toward the school, flashes of those lessons—how to spot a landmine, what signs to look for—kept racing through my mind. Was this it? It had to be. What else could it be? My chest ached, lungs burning from the sharp cold, as we burst inside and caught sight of the first teacher.

We all spoke at once, words tumbling over each other, broken by gasps for air. At first, she just stared, trying to piece together the mess we were spilling out. Then something in her eyes shifted—she understood. In a blink, she was gone, and almost immediately, the alarm split through the building.

Minutes blurred. Students poured outside, gathering in a tight mass in front of the school, pushed back from the field. Then came the military police—boots striking the ground—as they fanned out across the playground, the court, the trail. We stood frozen, watching, not knowing what would happen next.

We'd heard stories—mines at other schools, even daycare centers—but seeing it here, at our school, made my skin crawl. This was supposed to be the one safe place. We clung to that illusion because it gave us something to believe in: that even in war, children and learning would be spared.

But it wasn't true. It had never been. Not while bombs fell and sirens wailed. This was our life now—the endless question of safety, the constant reminder that nowhere was ever truly safe.

Within the hour, we were on a bus, driven somewhere away from the school. We all knew it was protocol, but it felt strange not to be allowed to simply go home. That was all any of us wanted—to run home, to our families. Instead, we sat in rows, carried off like passengers in someone else's plan.

Some of the boys laughed, calling it a free escape from class. Others sat pale, eyes far away, haunted by how close we'd come to exploding that day. The contrast almost made me laugh, too. I smirked, shook my head. We weren't the same anymore—not even among ourselves. Some of us were already numb.

I only felt dread. The bus felt smaller with every mile, like the air itself was pressing in, and all my sense of control was slipping away. Being a good student meant nothing here. School would always be haunting now.

Chapter Twenty-Two

CHAPTER TWENTY-TWO

Several hours later, we were back at school. The sun was slipping low, painting the sky in fading light and soft, beautiful hues. The air had grown cooler, and snow drifted down in quiet flakes, settling over the scene as if to soften what the day had done. By the bus stop, a small cluster of parents waited, their faces lit with relief or shadowed with worry.

I scanned the crowd for my own parents, but they weren't there. Ivana's mother was—I spotted her right away, eyes rimmed red, like she'd been crying. It hit me then: some parents must have been told, at least the ones who came. Most of us weren't met by anyone. That was typical, in its own way. Some kids had activities, others were expected at a friend's house, and plenty of parents were still at work. There were always reasons.

But the truth pressed in: no one had called. Not a single parent had been told what happened out there on that trail. We were still expected to shoulder it ourselves, to carry it home. So, we did—walking back in small groups or climbing onto the public buses, scattering into the city with the weight of the day hidden in our pockets, waiting for us to unfold it at the dinner table.

Chapter Twenty-Three

CHAPTER TWENTY-THREE

When I got home, Mom's worry showed in the way her eyes lingered on me, though she pretended to believe I'd been with friends or at folklore practice. She didn't press, but she knew. Mothers always do. Something in the way I carried myself—quieter, heavier—betrayed me.

I wanted to speak, but the words knotted in my throat. It wasn't just something that had happened at school. I had been part of it—and that made it different. That made it ours to bear, mine to express.

Ela trailed after me, eyes bright with the unspoken invitation to slip back into our imagined world. It wasn't play the way children usually played. It was something heavier, dreamlike—a place we built together to escape what waited outside our walls. But that afternoon, I felt apart from it, as if a pane of glass had come down between us. The weight I carried pressed against my chest. I knew I couldn't keep it in forever. Dinner would be the moment—when I'd finally speak it aloud and watch the ground shift beneath us.

At dinner, I let the words spill. I told them what had happened at school, how close it had come. Dad's face barely shifted, his expression steady, unreadable. But Mom's eyes brimmed almost at once. Tears slid down her cheeks in silence—no sudden gasp, no outburst—just the quiet surrender of a body that could no longer hold everything inside. She didn't ask me to stop, didn't rush to soothe or scold. She only listened, the worry in her chest bleeding out through her tears.

Our parents had a way of doing that—of swallowing the heavier things, holding them back until nightfall, when we were asleep, and they could unburden themselves in whispers we were never meant to hear.

When I finished, Dad finally spoke. "You trusted your instincts, and that kept you safe." His voice was even and steady, but softer now as his eyes lingered on me. He reached across the table, resting his hand over mine. "I'm glad you're safe." Then, without another word, he pulled me into a firm embrace, his arms saying what his voice never quite could.

He turned to Mom, adding gently, "I'll contact the school tomorrow. We'll get the details."

Mom nodded through her tears, caught between dread and relief. That was when Ela slid closer, her small voice cutting through the heaviness: "I'm so glad you saw it before it was too late. We'll be okay. We always are."

And I believed her, in that moment.

Chapter Twenty-Four

CHAPTER TWENTY-FOUR

The next few weeks settled into a rhythm we already knew too well—life suspended between fear and normalcy. Each day followed the same pattern: the distant hum of danger, the shadow of air raids, and then, somehow, the steady push of ordinary life pressing in.

For those of us not on the front lines, it was an invisible weight—an emotional burden that never quite lifted. Children still tried to be children, slipping into games and stolen laughter between sirens. Sometimes those small rebellions against fear made us feel less grown, less hardened, if only for an hour.

There were quiet conversations at kitchen tables and in dim stairwells: When would it end? Would we ever return to the way things were? Or would we finally get the chance to begin again—different, freer, something more hopeful than the fractured life we had known? No one knew. No one could say.

Still, we moved forward, step by step, to the steady, uneasy rhythm of a new normal.

Eventually, our parents decided we should move to the countryside to live with our grandparents. It was supposed to be safer, away from the city limits—as if open fields, farmland, and vineyards could somehow keep the darkness away. The area our grandparents lived in was a little safer, but it sat at a crossroads between large cities, which meant heavy military traffic and the usual wartime difficulties.

Maybe it was desperation to keep us safe, or maybe there were other motives we weren't told, but I could hear the despair in their voices. I wanted to protest, to say something—but the words wouldn't come, as if someone had stolen them right when I needed them most.

What would happen to Ivana and me? Would I ever see her again? The thought hit like a storm breaking over open water—sudden, violent, impossible to escape.

"I don't want to go," Ela whispered, breaking the silence.

Mom reached over, her voice soft, careful. "It won't be forever," she said, though I could hear the tremor beneath her words.

Chapter Twenty-Five

CHAPTER TWENTY-FIVE

We didn't leave right away. For weeks, the plan lingered in the air—unspoken but certain—like a storm cloud that refused to shift. Then one morning, without warning, it was simply time. Suitcases were packed, books stacked and left behind, small keepsakes chosen with the weight of final decisions. I watched Ela carefully tuck the old department store catalog into her bag—the one we'd spent hours poring over, page by page, letting its glossy images feed our imagined escape. To us, it wasn't just paper and ink. It was a kind of hope, something we didn't fully understand but clung to anyway. A single building block that, with our imagination, let us dream of a life bigger, brighter, and kinder than the one we knew.

Dad loaded everything into our little Renault, and before long, we were on the road. The city shrank in the rearview mirror, each turn pulling it farther away, and all we could do was watch it fall behind.

The next few weeks passed in a blur of new faces, a new school, and the strange effort of trying to make friends. It felt like slipping into someone else's shoes—familiar, but never quite a fit. We had always known this village through summers with our cousins, days spent running barefoot through fields and tumbling into vineyards until dusk called us home. But living here—walking to school every morning, sleeping under the same roof night after night—was different. It wasn't a holiday anymore. It was life.

And the countryside itself... it was beautiful in a way that hurt. Endless rows of corn and golden wheat swayed in the wind like waves, and the vineyards stretched wide, heavy with promise. The air smelled of damp soil and woodsmoke, clearer than anything we'd known in the city. At night, the sky opened with stars we'd never seen before. In the summers, that beauty had always felt like freedom. But now, under the weight of war, it felt fragile—temporary. A place pretending to be untouched while the world beyond it burned.

Winters in the village weren't busy or exciting. They passed in quiet rhythms—schoolwork, stories around the fire, endless games of cards. The wood stove burned almost constantly, its heat uneven but vital, while the cellar shelves held what our grandparents had carefully preserved from the last harvest: jars of pickled vegetables, rows of potatoes, whatever could last the season. Meals were simple and repetitive, but they filled us and kept us warm.

When the shelves began to thin, aid parcels from the UN and local forces filled the gaps—powdered milk, canned goods, enriched rice. They were meant to stretch what little we had, to remind us that survival, for now, was still possible.

The house felt cramped compared to our city apartment, but we had each other—and a few fragile comforts. No air raids, for one. The silence of that absence was almost surreal. We had lived so long on edge, waiting for sirens, waiting to flee, that stillness felt foreign. Here, we didn't have to brace for it every week.

But the war was never far. Enemy planes still cut across the sky, their engines droning overhead as they flew toward some distant destruction. It didn't matter if you were in the city or the countryside—the sound alone made dread seep into your bones. The only difference was that here, there were no local targets. Bombs rarely fell on these fields and vineyards.

At night, we sometimes saw illumination flares arc into the sky, casting ghostly light across the horizon. In a cruel, ironic way, it looked almost beautiful—like fireworks colliding with stars in some cosmic lightshow. But beneath that fleeting beauty, guilt always crept in. Because the truth was inescapable: that lightshow meant death. Someone beneath it wouldn't see morning. And in the dark, I couldn't stop wondering if one day, it might be Ivana.

Spring was finally on the horizon, and we could hardly wait to dive into it, like turning the page to a new chapter. There was something almost magical in watching life return—even when death and destruction still hovered around us. It felt like a promise that beauty could survive alongside the fear. More than anything, spring meant being outside again, breathing freely, feeling alive.

For me, the best part was always the flowers. Watching them push through the dirt as if nothing could stop them gave me something to look forward to—something beautiful to hold onto when the world felt so unpleasant. Especially the lilies. Always the lilies.

They were my favorite—not just for their beauty, but for their strength. Year after year, they weathered the storms, lying quiet beneath the frozen ground, only to rise again in full grace when spring returned. Their petals stood tall, serene and luminous, as if untouched by all the ruin around them.

To me, they were more than flowers. They were proof. Proof that survival could be elegant, that resilience could carry its own kind of beauty. And I held onto that with everything I had.

Chapter Twenty-Six

CHAPTER TWENTY-SIX

By April, spring had folded into Easter. It felt strange, celebrating resurrection when so much of life around us was marked by loss—but maybe that was the point. Hope came in pieces: a few painted eggs, the smell of bread rising in the oven, lilies nodding in the breeze. I clung to those fragments the way I clung to prayer—small, fragile things that somehow felt strong enough to hold us up.

That afternoon, Ela and I took our bikes down the trail that led to the forest near the house. The air was bright, the sunshine abundant, and for once, the village felt light with happiness. It seemed safe enough to wander, to stretch into the open. Riding fast, with the wind on my face, I felt a rare freedom—as if the world, for a moment, had given us permission to breathe again.

Ela had tied a red silk scarf around her neck, its edges trailing like a ribbon in the wind, while I wore my favorite bright floral top. We laughed as our pedals spun, our voices carrying across the fields.

"We could be Amanda and Biljana," I teased, "holidaying in the Italian countryside—or maybe the French Riviera. Glamorous, carefree, with nothing to weigh us down."

Ela grinned, her scarf snapping behind her. "We could be anywhere. That's what makes it fun—no one can tell us otherwise."

We slowed as the forest drew closer, the grass thick with wildflowers. I pointed toward a patch of poppies. "The sparkling mineral water will be our champagne," I said, mock elegant.

Ela laughed, playing along. "And the poppy seeds, our caviar."

We doubled over on our bikes, the kind of laughter that tumbled out unrestrained, hair wild in the wind. For that moment, we gave in completely. We rode the wave of fantasy, weaving our dreams into the gardens and vineyards, living in two worlds at once—the real and the imagined. It was effortless, intoxicating, pure joy, the kind that only sparks when you have no burdens to carry.

But reality has a way of cutting through. Dreams can only hold so much. From a distance, a familiar sound rose—the gut-wrenching thrum of engines overhead. My legs faltered.

"Lana!" Ela cried. "We need to hide!"

Chapter Twenty-Seven

CHAPTER TWENTY-SEVEN

At first, the hum sounded like farm equipment, and I thought maybe we were just overreacting. But then it deepened—fast, metallic, unmistakable. My heart dropped before my mind even named it. A jet. As the hum grew louder, the smell of burning fuel filled my lungs—thick, bitter, choking. I knew it was only seconds before it passed over us.

Panic took hold. *Run*, I told myself, the word burning through my chest like fire. "Ela! Run for the trench beside the forest!"

We let the bikes fall where they were and sprinted toward the tree line. But it was too late. We were just specks in an open field, and the sky knew it. The planes tore above us, so low the air collapsed—flattening us to the ground, the roar of engines shaking my ribs like a second heartbeat.

Then, almost before I could lift my head, came the chopping rhythm—the heavy, relentless thrum of blades.

A helicopter.

It swung into view, circling lower, taunting. The air cracked with bursts of fire, dirt spraying up around us in sharp spits. They weren't aiming to hit. They didn't have to. The message was clear: *we see you, we could end you, we want you afraid.*

Beside me, the red scarf fluttered wildly in the dirt—our ribbon of pretend glamour, our flag of joy—now just a target against the open green.

Ela's screams tore through the chopper's roar, and I gripped the grass until my knuckles turned white. It was all I could do—hold on—as we waited for the sky to finish its terror.

They called this psychological warfare on TV. I never really understood it until now. We'd heard about it from others, even seen it on the news, but this was the first time it found us—a deliberate game meant to terrorize civilians, to remind us how small we were beneath their wings.

I kept saying it over and over, like it could drown out the fear. *They won't kill us. Not today. Not when we finally started to feel free again.*

But the adrenaline twisted through me, sharp and sickening. My vision blurred. Nausea surged, and I closed my eyes, willing it to pass. It didn't. Everything thinned—the sound, the air, even my body—until I felt myself drifting again, suspended in time. Somewhere in between.

Chapter Twenty-Eight

CHAPTER TWENTY-EIGHT

Finally, the sounds faded into the distance, and I felt like I could breathe again. Ela and I just lay there, staring at each other—chests heaving as we tried to steady our breath and shed the tremors running through us.

Without a word, we walked back to our bikes and headed home. The picnic and the dream were over. For now.

On the ride back, we said nothing. The silence between us was heavy, filled with the echo of everything we couldn't name. I glanced down at my fingernails—caked with dirt—and thought, *Amanda would never have nails like this.* The irony of our pretend world pressed over me with a weight I didn't expect.

Was the fantasy still working? Was pretending even worth it? Would we ever escape this nightmare for real?

Hopelessness took hold of me like reins I couldn't control. It made me feel trapped, like there was no way out, and before I could stop myself, a sob broke loose.

"Sometimes it feels like we'll never get out of here alive," I whispered.

Ela ran to me and wrapped her arms around me—the kind of hug that softened the edges of the world just enough to bear. For once, I wasn't strong enough to be her anchor, but I let myself accept her comfort, knowing I was always safe with her.

Because no matter what was happening around us, somehow, we always found our way back to hope.

Hope to dream again.

Hope for a better world.

Maybe not now.

But maybe tomorrow.

That night, the silence in the house felt heavier than usual. The air still carried the faint smell of gunpowder from somewhere far away, and every creak of the floor made me flinch.

After dinner, I sat by the window, staring at the dark shapes of the trees against the fading light. My thoughts drifted, restless and heavy. The world outside felt smaller than ever—like all the color had drained from it.

Ela walked in quietly, the familiar catalog clutched in her hands.

"Lana," she said softly, "let's dream a little. It'll brighten your mood."

I turned toward her, ready to protest, but stopped when I saw her hopeful smile. Somehow, she still believed. Maybe that was her strength.

I managed a small smile and nodded. "It couldn't hurt," I whispered. Maybe it was foolish, maybe even childish, but letting go of the dream now felt like giving up the only part of ourselves still alive.

So we opened the catalog.

Page by page, we began to rebuild the world we'd imagined a hundred times—the one that once felt lost but somehow still waited for us—one silk dress, one shiny car, one shimmering piece of jewelry at a time, until we were so deep inside it that the noise, the fear, and even the night itself faded away.

For a while, we forgot where we were, and only the dream remained.

Chapter Twenty-Nine

CHAPTER TWENTY-NINE

Eventually, school and everyday life brought me back to something that resembled normalcy. Summer stretched long again, its warm evenings inviting us to linger outside with neighbors, stealing a few carefree hours at a time. The orchards behind the house glowed with light and fruit, and for brief moments, it felt like normal life was possible—even here. Sometimes it seemed as if the world itself was trying to remember how to breathe.

When the wind carried the right kind of silence, we could hear the convoys before we saw them—long, heavy columns of buses, armored vehicles, and tanks rumbling down the freeway beyond the fields. The earth trembled as they passed, shaking dust loose from our windowsills. Grandpa or Dad would fetch the binoculars, their movements quick and practiced, scanning the horizon to make sure the insignia was friendly. After they disappeared, we'd stand by the window for a moment, listening to the echo fade—a hollow quiet that made the world feel enormous and small at once.

As autumn came, the air filled with the scent of harvest. Festivals returned—small and humble, but enough to remind us of life before the war. It felt exciting again, like stealing moments of joy and peace, even if they only lasted a day or an hour. We welcomed them anyway. At the festivals, children played as if the war didn't exist—deliberately wishing it away, bringing the world before back to life, if only for an afternoon.

Still, there were nights when the sound of bombing shattered the distance—the local store, the pub. On those nights, terror gripped us all over again. But somehow, in the days that followed, life pulled us back into its rhythm. And so the cycle continued: fear, recovery, pretending, hope. Hope was stubborn like that—it came back even when no one invited it.

When school started again, it added another layer of distraction to our days. Lessons, laughter, and the quiet comfort of routine filled the hours, leaving less room for fear to settle in. There were new notebooks, sharpened pencils, and the soft hum of children trying to believe that learning still led somewhere. Walking home felt safer in daylight and in groups, though we never wore bright colors. We knew better than to stand out, in case the sky opened with a storm of engines again. Still, when the road curved past the orchard, the air smelled sweet, and sometimes we'd pause to taste the last of the fruit before winter claimed it.

For a while, the world almost felt steady—predictable, even. But underneath, I could sense something shifting, as if the ground itself were waiting to tell us what would come next. I didn't know it then, but the waiting was its own kind of storm.

Chapter Thirty

CHAPTER THIRTY

Winter arrived sooner than expected that year. Snow had quietly blanketed the fields around the village, casting a soft hush over everything and quieting the world in white. Those early snow days were always our favorite—a gentle kind of magic in the change of seasons, a shift in energy that reminded us something new was always waiting just beyond the horizon.

In those first days, we played outside until our faces went numb from the cold. The air felt fresher somehow, even in its harshness, carrying the faint scent of wood smoke from nearby chimneys. But soon, the snow became part of everyday life—a new normal, folded into the rhythm of our days. It wasn't that we minded; it just lost its initial hold on us.

Ela and I often talked about winters before the war—skiing and sledding trips with our parents in the mountains, steaming cups of tea by the fire, laughter echoing through warm lodges. War had taken that from us for two years now, so instead, we dreamed. Sometimes we imagined the day life would return to normal—when we could travel again, when freedom would feel real. Other times, we escaped into our fantasy world, picturing Amanda and Biljana draped in white wool and velvet, gliding through Alpine snow in luxury and ease. Dreaming, in any form, kept us tethered to hope.

Lately, though, something had shifted. Our parents were traveling back to the city more often than usual, their voices low and urgent when they returned. At night, after we'd gone to bed, I could still hear the quiet murmur of their conversations through the walls. The air on those nights felt different—sometimes lighter, sometimes heavier, as if the house itself couldn't decide whether to breathe easy or hold its breath, waiting for something unnamed.

Chapter Thirty-One

CHAPTER THIRTY-ONE

About a week before the holidays, another cease-fire was promised, so we traveled back to the city with our parents, thinking it would be just a quick visit. In some ways, it felt exciting to return, and the chance to see Ivana made me happy. Although Ela and I didn't really understand why they brought us along this time, we didn't question it. A change of scenery was exactly what we needed.

The city was alive with holiday lights, trying its best to summon the magic of the season. For the first time in months, the air felt gentle, as if it, too, wanted to believe in peace. Everyone seemed determined to create a sense of wonder for families, despite the war still lingering around them. There was always something special about the Christmas lights in the city—the way their brightness sparked joy and hope, no matter what was happening. We made our usual rounds through the market, enjoying roasted chestnuts, hot tea, and all the shimmer of the season.

We stopped at the cathedral, as always. The nativity scene stood beneath garlands of pine and gold ribbon, candlelight flickering against the marble. It was spectacular—exactly what we needed. A little family night out in the city.

We even visited our apartment. The spare room, with its chandelier and crystal vases, brought instant smiles to our faces—the room where we had built our world, our ballroom, and everything in between. A sanctuary that felt more like home than ever. It was bittersweet, though, because being there felt nostalgic, as if the walls themselves knew this moment wouldn't last. Not here. Not now. I longed for the day we could return—to be back with friends, to live without fear—but even that wish felt fragile, like my heart already sensed a shift in the air.

After the apartment, Dad announced we were going out to eat at a nearby restaurant—one of the few still open during cease-fires and holidays. The options were limited, but it was something we always looked forward to. Ela's face lit up, her excitement filling the room. I wanted to linger a little longer in our ballroom—the last bit of glimmer left in this world. I had the strangest urge to say goodbye to it, though I didn't yet understand why.

We walked to the restaurant, just a block from the apartment—the one with the little green awning and large front windows. Ela and I had passed it hundreds of times, though we'd only eaten there a few times before. Going out to eat was rare these days, so when it happened, it felt extra special.

Its windows glowed with a soft amber light that spilled into the snowy street. Inside, the air smelled of freshly baked bread, and the low murmur of conversation felt almost like music. For a moment, it was easy to forget everything beyond those walls.

We were seated in a quiet spot near the back of the restaurant. Ela and I exchanged glances, both wishing we'd been closer to the front windows, where we could watch the world go by. But Dad seemed to prefer the back. *Safety*, we thought. He was keeping us away from the glass in case of an unexpected attack. My mind accepted that explanation easily enough, and I let myself settle into the moment.

This little corner place was known for its pizza, and Ela and I instantly knew that's what we wanted—along with nectar juice that, by some miracle, was actually in stock. It felt like we'd won the lottery. That kind of luck didn't come often during wartime, and it filled us with a joy I couldn't quite put into words. All we could do was giggle and smile.

Mom noticed the quiet moments between us and gave us the biggest smile we'd seen from her in years. For a brief moment, everything felt right. It wasn't a grand occasion, but in its own way, it was perfect—and we felt like we were on top of the world.

When the food arrived, we ate quietly at first. There was comfort in the simple act of it—in warm plates, clinking silverware, and the illusion of peace. Then Dad set his fork down. He looked at Mom for a long moment, and something unspoken passed between them.

He cleared his throat softly.

"Girls," he said, his voice calm but heavy, "your mother and I have something important to tell you."

Ela stopped mid-bite. "What is it?"

Mom reached across the table, her fingers brushing mine. "We're leaving," she said gently.

Dad's voice followed, steady and certain. "We're moving to New York City."

For a moment, I thought I'd misheard them. The words hung between us, suspended in the air like the breath we hadn't taken yet.

Ela blinked. "New York?" she whispered. "As in... America?"

Dad nodded. "Yes. We leave in less than a week."

"But... why so soon?" I asked, my voice caught between disbelief and hope.

Dad sighed. "Because everyone is trying to leave, and it's not easy to get out. We can't risk waiting. If people find out, we could become targets."

Mom added softly, "It has to happen quietly, while there's still time."

Ela's eyes were wide, glistening. "We're really going?"

Dad smiled faintly. "Yes. It's time for a new start. A safer life. You'll see."

The table fell quiet again, but it wasn't the uneasy silence from before—it was a stillness full of everything we couldn't say.

My heart swelled with joy and ache all at once. I thought of our apartment, our friends, our grandmother's kitchen, and the orchard in winter. How do you say goodbye to an entire world in a matter of days?

Ela reached for my hand under the table, squeezing it tightly. Her smile trembled, caught somewhere between excitement and fear.

"Lana..." she said softly, her voice barely above the hum of the restaurant. "Do you think... maybe we'll become them?"

I looked at her—the reflection of the candlelight in her eyes, the snow falling quietly beyond the glass.

Inside me, something shifted: a quiet warmth that felt danger-ously close to hope.

And for a moment, it didn't feel impossible.

EPILOGUE

The golden sunset glowed through the windows of JFK International Airport as I made my way toward the gate. Beams of light shimmered against the glass, turning the crowds into moving silhouettes. My designer carry-on rolled beside me, its leather catching the light—proof that even impossible things can quietly find their way into being. I reached the gate just in time for the first-class boarding call to Milan.

I pulled up my boarding pass as the attendant announced the call for first-class passengers. I'd tried calling Ela earlier, but it had gone to voicemail, so I sent a text instead—a small note to say I was here, that the flight was on time. Still no response.

The gate agent scanned my pass and smiled, his voice warm and professional. "Have a wonderful flight, Ms. Tomaš."

I made my way to seat 3A—my preferred spot on the plane—where soft lighting glowed over brushed metal and cream upholstery, a calm elegance in motion. I slid my bag beneath the seat just as my phone buzzed.

Teo:

Have a safe flight. I'll see you when you land.

I smiled at the simplicity of it—the kind of message that felt like steady ground, like something that had always been part of our orbit.

Before I'd even locked my phone, the flight attendant appeared with a smile and a chilled flute of champagne. "Thank you for flying with us again, Lana," she said, her tone warm with recognition. I smiled back and accepted the glass, the bubbles catching the last trace of sunset through the window.

My phone buzzed again, and for a moment, I thought it might be Ela. But the message was from Beth, the event coordinator we'd come to know well.

Beth:

Hi Lana, just wanted to confirm that you're all set for The Vue in March. Can't wait to see you and Ela there—it's going to be spectacular!

I smiled, pulling up my calendar to confirm the date. Between meetings and travel, the weeks were already filling fast—and scattered among them was the one recurring appointment I wished I didn't need. A quiet reminder that some echoes of the past can still interrupt even the brightest of days.

A few moments later, my phone buzzed again. This time, it was Ela.

Sorry I missed your call—Lara's case kept me in court longer than expected.

She's terrified her recital will suffer this weekend.

Wish you could make it.

It's been a long week.

I had another nightmare last night. We didn't make it to the shelter in time. But then I woke up to the sunrise over the city and realized it was just a dream. Or a memory. I can't tell anymore.

But I'm grateful it's this world I woke up to.

I read the message twice, my fingers tracing the cool rim of the glass. Outside the window, the light over the tarmac shifted from gold to dusk, and the engines began to hum. For a moment, the world felt suspended—quiet, almost merciful.

I took a slow sip of champagne, letting the taste linger as the plane readied for takeoff.

And in that moment of weightless stillness, I wondered—not for the first time—whether anyone ever truly leaves the shadows of the past, or if we only learn to live somewhere in between.

AUTHOR'S NOTE

Somewhere in Between was shaped by the spaces I've spent much of my life trying to understand—the places where memory, imagination, fear, beauty, and resilience all coexist.

We spent part of our childhood in Croatia while the war moved around us in uneven, unpredictable rhythms. We weren't on the front lines, and the city we lived in wasn't under constant siege. But we were still in a war zone—a place where danger arrived without warning, and silence didn't always mean safety. That time shaped us quietly and deeply, even as it unfolded alongside the brighter chapters of our childhood. I've always felt it was important to honor that truth: that every family's experience of that time in Croatia was different, and that the war revealed many forms of suffering, resilience, and courage.

The bond I shared with my sister became one of the great constants of my childhood—a friendship formed by circumstance and strengthened by tenderness, persistence, and a shared instinct to find light wherever we could. We carried each other through that time in ways we didn't fully understand then, but feel the depth of now.

Part Two carries the echo of that real New Year's Eve—a moment when the world tilted, and I felt, for an instant, as if I'd fallen out of it. Its quiet shadow stayed with me, shaping the way I came to understand fear, resilience, and the fragile space we learn to inhabit somewhere in between.

In that uncertain space, we turned to imagination the way children often do—instinctively, without question—creating worlds that felt brighter and safer than the one outside our windows. We borrowed pieces of beauty wherever we could find them, stitching together futures filled with color, comfort, and possibility. Those imagined worlds lived alongside the real one—not replacing it, but giving us something to reach toward, something that whispered life could one day be different. Imagination became its own kind of resilience—a quiet, steady place where hope could breathe. It taught us that even in difficult times, children carry an astonishing ability to hold fear in one hand and possibility in the other. That space between the two was where we lived, and it was where we learned to endure—together.

Writing this novella allowed me to return to that space with a new understanding. As adults, we learn that trauma doesn't vanish; it settles into us in gentle and persistent ways. Healing is not about erasing the past—it's about learning to live with it, to carry it with tenderness instead of fear. We move forward, but the past moves with us. Somewhere in that overlap, between what was and what is, we find the shape of who we become.

This story is fiction, shaped by the emotional resonance of a brief time in my childhood. Some moments echo real memories, carried into the narrative in altered or refined form; others spring from imagination alone. It speaks to the in-between spaces my sister and I once occupied, and to the way hope eventually widened our world. Croatia is my home and my heritage—a place of lasting beauty—and this note touches only the short season shadowed by war.

More than anything, this book honors the resilience of children, the power of imagination, and the complicated beauty of surviving something that never fully leaves you. It's about the worlds we create to protect ourselves, the friendships that hold us steady, and the way those imagined worlds sometimes lead us toward the ones we finally get to live in.

If this story resonated with you, even in some small in-between place, I'm honored to have shared that space with you.

— Lilly Benton

ACKNOWLEDGMENTS

This story came into the world because of the people who supported me, uplifted me, and never stopped believing in what it could become.

To my sister, Kristina—the co-author of every world we ever dreamed our way into. You were my first home, my first friend, and the keeper of our shared imagination. This story is stitched with the threads of our childhood, our resilience, and every dream we once chased together. Thank you for cheering me on, encouraging me, and believing in this book from the very beginning. I share this moment with you.

To my husband, Andrew—thank you for your love, your steadiness, and the way you believe in me even when I stumble. You gave me the space to write, to heal, and to build something I once thought impossible. Your encouragement carried me through every doubt.

To my brother, Alan—thank you for your steady encouragement, for listening with patience and curiosity, and for reminding me that this story could be something real. Your support helped carry me to the finish line.

To my beta readers—Mary Evora, Karen Frederick, Hayley Galvin, Jennifer Lima, and Kristina Tkalec—your insight, generosity, and thoughtful reflections helped shape this story into its truest form. Thank you for giving your time and your hearts to these pages. Your feedback was invaluable.

To everyone who has supported me, encouraged me, or believed in me along the way—thank you. Independent publishing is an act of faith, and I am endlessly grateful for every person who helped me take this leap.

And finally, to the little girl I once was—flipping through a catalog in a dimly lit room, imagining her way toward a brighter world:

You made it.

And this book is for you.

ABOUT THE AUTHOR

Ljiljana "Lilly" Benton is a debut author whose work blends memory and imagination into lyrical, emotionally resonant fiction. Her writings explore universal themes of resilience, identity, and the hidden truths beneath the surface of our lives—echoes that often linger long after the final page.

Born in Croatia, Lilly now lives in the Lake Norman area of North Carolina with her husband, Andrew, and their two dogs, Bon Bon and Watson. She works in accounting while pursuing her passion for storytelling alongside her professional career.

Her debut novella, *Somewhere in Between*, introduced readers to her distinctive voice and character-driven style. She is currently developing additional works set in the same world, along with new standalone projects that deepen her exploration of short literary fiction.